S'GANA The Black Whale

S'GANA

THE BLACK WHALE

Sue Stauffacher

Alaska Northwest Books™
Anchorage • Seattle

To my parents, Joan and Al Stauffacher, for their support and encouragement.

And to my loving husband, Roger, with whom all things are possible.

Library of Congress Cataloging-in-Publication Data
Stauffacher, Sue, 1961–
    S'gana, the black whale / by Sue Stauffacher.
        p.   cm.
    Summary: While spending the summer with his grandparents in Wisconsin, twelve-year-old Derek discovers his Haida Indian heritage which draws him to a distressed black whale at a local marine park.
    ISBN 0-88240-396-6
    [1. Killer whales—Fiction.   2. Whales—Fiction.   3. Haida Indians—Fiction.   4. Indians of North America—Fiction.   5. Grandparents—Fiction.]   I. Title.
PZ7.S8055Sg   1992
[Fic]—dc20
                                                        92-17573
                                                        CIP
                                                        AC

Project editor: Ellen Harkins Wheat
Editor: Brenda Peterson
Cover and book design: Alice Merrill Brown
Cover illustration: Christine Cox

Alaska Northwest Books™
A division of GTE Discovery Publications, Inc.
22026 20th Avenue S.E.
Bothell, WA 98021

Printed on recycled acid-free paper in the United States of America

Table of Contents

Note to Readers

While I have tried to remain true to the spirit of Haida beliefs, this novel is a work of fiction and is not meant to portray Haida culture or mythology precisely.

One

The Legend

Listen, children. I will tell you this story only once. Long ago at Masset, on an Island of Haida Gwaii or Land-of-Our-People, there lived a young Indian boy named Ilyea. He was Raven Clan, tall and strong and dark as the inlet waters. Ilyea lived in the time before tragedy struck our people. His days were busy with purpose—hunting salmon and playing with the other children in the village.

The Power-of-the-Shining-Heaven made the Haida Gwaii full of riches for our people. There were alder trees, firs and spruces, hemlocks and cedars. We used these trees to build our canoes, our houses, and our crest poles, to weave our rain capes, and to smoke our fish. There were crab apples and wild berries for gathering. The grouse and the teal also gave themselves to us.

From the ocean we had more riches. Many kinds of salmon, halibut, cod, and herring offered themselves to us, as well as the sea lion, sea otter, and shellfish.

There were Ocean People who did not give themselves to us. One was our brother, the black whale. Black Whale People are very powerful. We shared the ocean and its riches with those who lived in the Village-Below-the-Sea.

Ilyea was much like Raven. He loved to play tricks on others, especially his mother, Kitkune. Ilyea had not yet learned to respect the Power-of-the-Shining-Heaven.

"The world is as sharp as a knife," his mother would warn him.

"But it is *my* knife," Ilyea would say, laughing and tugging her long braid.

One day Ilyea and his brother Ikwe prepared their canoe to go look for salmon. Their father had gone to another camp because at Masset the fish were playing tricks and making themselves hard to find. Kitkune begged her sons not to go.

"A storm approaches. Soon Thunderbird Hilina will awake and rustle his great cloud wings. When he opens his eyes, beams of lightning will shoot from the sky."

But Ilyea just laughed. "Hilina does not scare me.

Ikwe and I will find where the Salmon People are hiding." He reminded his mother that it was late in the summer and the village had only twenty baskets of dried fish.

Kitkune tried to convince them not to go, but she knew her son was right. The fish were badly needed.

Now at this time S'gana, the black whale, was playing in the Village-Below-the-Sea with her young sons. When she leapt out of the water, she saw the sons of Kitkune approach.

Long ago, S'gana's mother had told her about Kitkune's coming to this island. The villagers had watched the strange child, dressed in the long rain cape and woven hat of their people, drift slowly ashore in a canoe. She had no paddles with her and no memory of her life before. When they tried to help her from the boat, Kitkune shook her head. She would not move until the villagers sang "the Black Whale Maid arrives." The chief of the village saw Kitkune as a sign from the Power-of-the-Shining-Heaven, and so he brought her into his family and made her his daughter.

One day, Kitkune went with her brothers on a sea lion hunt. They came upon S'gana's whale mother thrashing wildly, a spear stuck in her side. Kitkune swam to the frightened whale and climbed onto her back. Singing softly in whale tongue, Kitkune calmed her and worked the spear free.

Now, here was S'gana, the great black whale, watching Kitkune's sons approach. S'gana swam quickly to the side of their boat. She also knew of the storm and wished to warn Ilyea of the dangers to young boy people. She leapt up and over the boat and swam back toward the inlet.

"I have no time for games now, S'gana," Ilyea called, as he and Ikwe cut a path through the dark waves.

But Ikwe became frightened. "We are going too far, brother," he said. "Hilina is waking and rolling over. See how the clouds rush in."

Ilyea ignored his brother. He wanted to be a great hunter like S'gana was in the Village-Below-the-Sea. Then the tribe would have much dried fish in winter and would know that he, Ilyea, was the greatest salmon hunter of all.

"S'gana is warning us to turn back," Ikwe called to his brother over the sound of the breaking waves.

"She's just playing," Ilyea laughed, as his paddle cut the rough water. "She doesn't want us to know her salmon fishing place."

When the storm came, the Sacred-One-Standing-and-Moving shook the earth so that terrible waves rose up around them. The boys struggled for a long time to keep the canoe upright and to make their way home, but it was hopeless.

The Power-of-the-Shining-Heaven closed his great eyes and the sky went dark. Ilyea saw his mistake too late. Now his brother would die because of his own selfish pride. Silently he asked the Power-of-the-Shining-Heaven to spare Ikwe.

"Take me alone," he prayed. When a flash of lightning tore through the sky and a sea otter appeared at the side of his boat, Ilyea knew that all was agreed.

"Put up your paddle, Ikwe," Ilyea called to his frightened brother. "I have struck a bargain with the Power-of-the-Shining-Heaven, who will see you to safety." He told his brother to lie down in the bottom of the canoe and he placed their paddles beside him.

"Quiet your mind, brother, and let the waves carry you. When Hilina has moved on, you can paddle home." Ilyea laid his hand on his brother's shoulder, then dove into the churning sea.

Far away on the shore Kitkune knew at once what had happened. She sank to the ground. "Power-of-the-Shining-Heaven," she cried, "let not my heart be sorry. Save my sons from the Village-Below-the-Sea."

She ran to the water's edge, where her cries became a sad and beautiful song. The song was the same one she had sung on that day long ago when she pulled the spear from S'gana's mother's back. Now Kitkune understood. She would ask S'gana to save her sons, and she would sing until they came safely back to her.

In the Village-Below-the-Sea, S'gana listened carefully to Kitkune's song, and set out to find Ilyea. She reached him just as his spirit made ready to leave his body for the last time. Swimming beneath him, S'gana made her back into an island for Ilyea.

For three days S'gana stayed at the surface, balancing Ilyea on her smooth black back. Her whale sons brought salmon to keep up her strength, but she would not eat. As long as she heard the distant song of Kitkune coming to her through the water, S'gana felt no hunger.

For three days Kitkune sang, refusing to eat or rest. When the Sacred-One-Standing-and-Moving had calmed the sea, Ikwe returned. He told his mother that Ilyea had given his spirit for him. But Kitkune did not believe his words.

At dusk on the third day, three black whales appeared at the mouth of the bay. The villagers shook their heads sadly, for they knew the black whales swam close to shore only when someone had drowned. But then they heard the sound of arms slapping against the water and Ilyea calling to them as he came ashore to greet his mother. When Kitkune finished singing her song of thanksgiving, the whales leapt out of the water and dove deeply. Then they swam toward the mouth of the bay and back to their homes in the Village-Below-the-Sea.

Ilyea learned to respect the Power-of-the-Shining-Heaven and lived to an old age. He became the tribe's greatest salmon hunter—not because of his Raven-like cunning, but because of his friendship with S'gana, who led him to the Salmon People every year.

As our people know, the spirit is reborn five times. After the fifth time, it becomes like the earth, knowing nothing. When at last Ilyea died, his spirit passed to Kwawlang, and from Kwawlang to Pahl, and then to Kilgulans, and after Kilgulans to Kwung.

There was at this time terrible disease and much sorrow for our people; many died and there were few bodies for the spirits to return to. After Kwung, Ilyea's spirit was without a body for some time. Finally, a child was born who was only a quarter Haida. Since every spirit seeks to return to the earth, Ilyea's spirit chose this boy, son of Wiba and Ronald Simpson. He was not born on the Haida Gwaii or near it. He was not even given a Haida name. He was called Derek.

Two

The Empty Box

Derek Simpson was leaving home for the summer. There was no doubt about that. His mother refused to listen to his arguments.

"You'll be doing your grandparents a favor," she replied, when Derek suggested he might be getting in their way. "Tani tells me that Joe needs a companion. You two can go fishing."

Fishing with his grandfather was not something he looked forward to doing. For starters, Joe couldn't catch a fish if you gave him the ocean for a net. Plus, gutting and cleaning the fish gave Joe the willies. That meant Derek would have to do it.

Derek could think of only one reason why he was being sent away from his home in Port Espadon, Washington, to Arcadia, a small farming town in the middle of Wisconsin. His mom wanted him out of the way.

Ever since his parents had gotten divorced, he'd lived in an apartment with his mom. Derek thought living in an apartment was all right. There was a pool and lots of sidewalks for skateboarding—though if the manager caught you, he'd call your parents and complain. But his mom wanted a house again. She'd even promised him a dog if they got one, so he figured he wanted a house, too.

In the spring, Derek's mother had bought the only house they could afford. It was a run-down, quirky old house that promised all kinds of surprises from the outside. On the inside, though, wallpaper hung in long curls, linoleum bubbled up from the countertops, and the carpet smelled like the neighborhood tomcat had marked it as his territory.

But Derek's mother never saw these drawbacks. She walked through the rooms smiling and saying, "Our hanging plants are going to get so much more sun here." In the backyard, which was choked with weeds and tangled prickly bushes, she put her arm around her son and said, "We'll have a garden just like Tani's back here. You'll have to get your grandma to teach you how to care for one."

To save money, Derek's mother had decided to move into the house by herself over the summer. She was worried about leaving Derek alone while she worked and attended night classes at the university to complete her degree.

She told Derek that he had to go live with his grandparents for the summer so she could give him a better life. But sometimes Derek wondered if she just wasn't too busy for him. He was twelve now. He could help fix things up. When he told his mom what he could do, she said, "Who would look after you?" He wanted to say, "Who's going to look after you, then?" Wasn't he the one who was supposed to do that after his dad left?

But Derek could see it was no use arguing with her. Being half Indian made his mom "stubborn as a tree trunk," according to Dad. Once she made up her mind to do a thing, it was halfway done.

Now Derek had new worries. His grandma was all Indian, which could make her twice as stubborn as his mom. But to be fair, Derek had never noticed that about her before. And his Grandpa Joe, his mom said, was like Raven, the trickster; sometimes it was hard to tell if he was joking or serious.

That was about all Derek knew about his grandparents. He rarely saw them, except during the short visits Tani and Joe made to Washington. Derek's mother told him that Tani had bad memories of the Northwest.

Tani's brother, Kwung, had spent time in jail and later was shot in a fight. Tani's mother had died soon afterward. But when Derek asked to know more, his mother said he would understand better when he was older.

When it came time to pack, Derek couldn't decide what to put in the box that his mother was to send him later. He was supposed to choose books, games, or toys he would miss too much to part with for a whole summer. But the night before Derek was to leave, the box was still empty.

"There's nothing you want besides clothes?" his mother asked.

"My skateboard's going in my carry-on bag."

"And that's it?"

"What would *you* bring if you had only one box and all your stuff to consider?" Derek asked her.

"I'd bring the button blanket passed down to me from Tani for luck, my silver locket from your father, and a conch shell to remind me of the ocean." Derek's mother spoke quickly, as if she had already given the matter some thought. Then, taking him by the shoulders, she brought her face down to his. Derek found he couldn't look back at her, so he settled on looking at the creases around her mouth. He could see them even though she wasn't smiling. For some reason, that made him sad. "And I'd roll you tight inside the blanket and bring you, too."

"Then *you* get in the box," Derek said, meaning it as a joke, but feeling like he might cry right then. His mother must have seen the change because she grabbed him and held him tight against her. After a while, she stood and picked up the box.

"I'll take care of this," she said. "I'll surprise you."

He hadn't meant to be stubborn about the box, but how could he tell her? The ocean doesn't fit into a box. Neither do seagulls or foghorns or killer whales. How could he tell her the only time he felt right was when he sat on Hansen's bluff, looking out over the ocean, or when he listened to whales vocalize as they passed through the strait? How could he tell her he was afraid that when he returned, those feelings would be gone forever?

If Derek had considered himself a normal boy, he might not have dreaded the trip so much. After all, most of his friends were busy over the summer and his grandfather did collect old cars and have his own wood-working shop. But Derek had a secret he could not tell anyone, not even his mother or his best friend, Michael.

Ever since he was little, Derek had felt at times that he was not one, but two people. During his art class, for instance, the teacher had told them to paint a landscape. But when he closed his eyes and tried to imagine his favorite view of the ocean and the shoreline, he couldn't recognize what he was seeing. It was almost like watching a movie in his head of a place he'd never been before. The land curved sharply around the water and he thought he saw smoke rising from the shore and tall dorsal fins cutting through the ocean waves.

Then from a distance, he saw himself just the way he was, getting ready to dip his brush into his watercolor set. And the one who watched him was laughing. "What is a painting?" he said to Derek. "It does not compare with the Island."

What island? The whole thing lasted only a moment. The two Dereks melted together as Ms. Woerner rustled past him in her painter's smock, handing out supplies. Now who would ever believe a story like that?

In dreams, Derek visited the Island with his other self many times. Though he had never seen the carved tree trunks that stood at the front of the houses or fish drying over a low fire, it all seemed so familiar. When he awoke, the visions disappeared as rapidly as mist at sunrise, but his senses recalled everything—the chill fog penetrating his skin, the tangy smell of cedar and salt, the slow, regular spouting of whales.

On his last night in Port Espadon, Derek lay awake for a long time thinking about this secret life. The only time the boy inside him seemed happy was when Derek went down to the shore. What would *that* Derek do when the walking-around-every-day normal Derek moved to a place that was all cornfields and dairy farms, more than eight hundred miles from the nearest ocean—and not even the right ocean?

Three

The Gold Card

The plane landed in Madison, Wisconsin, in the late afternoon. When Derek entered the airport, he saw his grandmother, Tani Roberts, before she saw him. Tani stood at the end of a line of people who were looking around with anticipation, careful smiles painted on their faces. Her face showed nothing. She could have been standing in a supermarket checkout line.

"You and Tani both act like you have nothing to say," he remembered his mom saying once. "But to look at you, a person would think you were keeping a secret." He'd wondered if there were two Tanis as well, one who was the normal-walking-around Tani and one who was always laughing.

Derek stayed out of his grandmother's sight as long

as he could, watching her. She was short and round with big, full arms sticking out of a flowered top. Her shirt wasn't tucked in. It hung over her waist and skirt. Her rope sandals barely held her wide brown feet. Derek caught sight of her long dark braid streaked with gray as she flicked her head to follow another young boy with her eyes.

When she did see him, Tani smiled, her face creasing the way his mom's did, only deeper. After an airplane ride full of strangers asking him personal questions like "So, have you got a girlfriend?" he was happy to see his grandma's quiet face. He wanted to throw his arms around her, but by the time she reached him, he changed his mind. When she pulled him against her warm, soft body, he stiffened.

"Too big to hug?" was all she said.

"Where's Grandpa?"

"Home fixing the TV." With her arm around his shoulder, Tani guided Derek through the crowds of people. "I took out a tube. Just wanted to see how long it would take him to figure it out." This much Derek remembered about his grandparents—they were always playing tricks on one another.

He and Tani walked through the crowded airport in silence.

It wasn't until they reached the baggage carousel

that he asked how they were going to get home. Tani didn't drive.

"Clem Hutchins, a friend of ours," Tani answered. "He's waiting outside with his car." Derek was disappointed. He didn't want to meet any new people.

"How's Wiba?" Tani asked, using his mother's Haida name.

"Okay, I guess."

"Okay, I guess? You practicing to be a politician?" Derek wasn't sure what that meant, but he could tell Tani wasn't satisfied with his answer. He grabbed at his battered old suitcase, the one that belonged to his mother when she was a kid. Derek had insisted on bringing it, even though the man at the counter made them tie it up with twine so it wouldn't burst. He pulled his suitcase off the conveyor belt and started walking away.

"That's it?" Tani was bent over, watching the suitcases appear from behind the black curtains as if by magic.

"My mom's sending a box," Derek called over his shoulder, and kept on walking.

Outside, a man in a red bow tie and red suspenders pulled up next to them and got out of an old station wagon.

"Clem always gets dressed up for the airport," Tani

explained as they got in the car.

"What is it boys your age like to do?" Clem asked Derek after they had gotten on the freeway. "Bet you like to fish."

"Not really." Derek had decided on the airplane that honesty was the best policy when it came to fishing.

"Joe doesn't like to fish, either." Tani tugged Derek's sleeve from the back seat. "He just says he does because he thinks you do."

"Well, we were hoping you'd help us with our toy making," Clem said. "Joe's got us in over our heads on Christmas orders." As Clem explained how he and Joe had turned Joe's workshop into a toy factory, Derek looked out the window at the rolling checkerboard hills of farm country. *Welcome to Arcadia,* a large green sign declared. "Trouble is, we end up giving away so many hobby horses and toy trains that we never make any money," Clem complained. "Your grandpa has a soft spot for kids. Now, I can take 'em or leave 'em." He winked at Derek, who mostly kept his eyes on the road.

After Clem dropped them off, Joe ran down the walk to greet them. He stepped in front of Tani, running his long fingers through a full head of hair. "That was very funny about the TV tube," he said.

"Take you long to figure out?"

"Long as it did to open up the back." Joe took Derek's face in both his hands and pressed hard. "How was your flight, Derek?" Derek stared for a moment at the sunburned strip that always ran along his grandfather's long nose. Before he could answer, Tani said, "So you found it was gone, but do you know where I hid it?" She marched into the house, her braid swinging back and forth behind her.

"Grandpa Joe?"

"Just call me Joe, Derek," he said as he led his grandson into the house. "Don't worry about Tani. She'll get hers." Then he ran up the stairs, taking them two at a time, yelling, "I can smell it already!"

Derek was left in the hallway holding his suitcase. He wasn't sure what to do since he'd only visited this house once before. The familiar smell of cedar comforted him. Joe had built almost all the furniture out of cedar. Tani used the leftover wood chips for packing material, so whenever Derek opened up a book they sent him, he could smell cedar on every page.

He glanced around the corner to the kitchen. Whoever built this house wasn't very practical. As he explored the downstairs, Derek found deep, odd-shaped closets you could almost camp out in, and an outside stairway from the ground to the second floor. There were three bathrooms and three tubs, and all the tubs stood above the floor on feet that looked like eagles' claws. On the walls hung old farm tools, and there was a sofa or a bed in every room except the kitchen. Later, Tani explained that Joe was so lazy he needed a place to lie down no matter where he was.

When Tani came back downstairs, her braid was loose and her shirt was pulled back where Joe had grabbed her as they ran up the stairs. His grandparents were as weird as this house. They still wrestled.

"What, still here?" she said, pulling her blouse forward and fixing herself a little while Derek studied the buckles on his suitcase. "Did Joe forget to tell you where you sleep?"

"Or you did."

Tani put her arm around Derek and led him into the kitchen. "Things will go a lot easier for you if you take my side in these matters," she said, throwing open the refrigerator. "All the fresh strawberries you want. Later this summer there will be raspberries and blackberries, too." She got out a bowl, spooned strawberries into it, poured on cream, and sprinkled the whole thing with sugar.

"You sleep wherever you want, in a bed, on the floor, whatever." Tani smiled. Derek put his suitcase down and took the spoon from her hand. He knew exactly where he would sleep.

"I found it," Grandpa Joe called down from the top of the stairs. "You left a trail a mile wide."

Tani looked at Derek and shrugged. "Big deal. A blind man could have found that tube. I just hope he didn't lie down on the bed before he looked under the mattress."

When Derek was finished, he rinsed his bowl in the sink, grabbed his suitcase, and went upstairs. The old nursery was just off the stairway on the far side of the house and he had to go past a laundry chute, a bathroom, and down a long hallway before he got to the next bedroom. It was just a small room with a day bed and a crib, but one wall of it was almost all windows, which Derek liked. The best part of all was that it had a private door to the outside that locked and a stairway that led down to the walk in back of the house.

Derek set his suitcase on the bed and sat next to it, feeling the springs through the thin pad and smelling the damp, old smell of the bedcovers. Tani and Joe showed up in the doorway, holding hands. They seemed to have forgotten about the TV tube. Derek just hoped they knew how to put it back.

"Smart choice." Joe sat down next to Derek and elbowed him in the side. "We'll never know what time you get home from your dates." Derek pulled at the twine on his suitcase. He took off his shoes and socks and felt the cool wooden floor beneath his toes.

"You'll have all the privacy you need here," Joe went on. "We can't hear a thing this far down the hall. That's why Tani made it the nursery. So your mother's crying wouldn't wake her up." That got him a slap on the arm from Tani, so he changed the subject. Reaching into his pocket, Joe pulled out a small, gold card and handed it to Derek. It was printed in black with the outline of a killer whale in the middle. "Ocean Park Gold Card Member," it said.

"They built an aquarium and a marine life park here a couple months back," Joe explained. "We all wondered why they'd bring whales and dolphins to the middle of farm country, but the paper said it was so people far away from either ocean could learn about them. I've been there a couple of times, but Tani, she won't go."

Derek glanced up at Tani. She was looking out the window. She had that distracted look that means you're inside your head somewhere, somewhere far away. He never liked to be caught doing it himself because he was afraid he'd have to explain. And he hated to lie. He went back to studying his card.

"With this card, you can get in anytime you want. All summer. I'd like you to have it, Derek, 'cause I know how much you love the ocean."

Derek set the card down carefully and rubbed his palm on his pants. Then he held his hand out to his grandfather. "Thanks," he said, and they shook hands. Derek looked up at Tani.

"Don't thank *me*," she said, turning around and walking out the door. "It's from your grandpa."

Derek wanted to ask her what was the matter with it, but he knew better.

"All right if I unpack now?"

"Sure." Joe got up slowly, pushing off from the bed. "I'll take the crib out of your way." But he had trouble handling it by himself, so Derek helped him carry it down to the basement. It was the first time he had thought about Joe being old. They always acted so much like kids, Derek had never imagined his grandparents getting old and dying.

Back in his room, Derek hung up his clothes in the closet and put his T-shirts and underwear in an old dresser. When he was down to the bottom of his suitcase, he moved the area rug closer to the bed so he could sit with his back propped up against it. From one of his suitcase pockets, he got out several packets of old baseball cards, including some that he'd taken from his mom's collection.

Derek had to admit he'd left the box empty partly to make his mom feel bad. He'd packed other important things under his clothes or in the suitcase pockets, like his Swiss Army knife and a picture of his mom as a little girl. She was sitting on a hillside somewhere on the Washington coast, looking out over the ocean.

Derek chose the packet with his favorite team players from the early seventies. Since his home team, the Seattle Mariners, wasn't in place then, Derek decided he would pick from the best players in the league at that time to make up a winning Mariners team. For a moment, he considered asking for Joe's help, since his grandpa might remember some of the players, but then he decided against it. All he could remember Joe ever talking about was the Green Bay Packers and their coach, the great Vince Lombardi.

Of course, it was unbelievable that he could get all his first picks, so Derek allowed himself only two top choices from both the American and National Leagues. From the American League, he was considering Reggie Jackson. Reggie could bat fourth and play right field. He looked over Reggie's stats again, and the small numbers started to blur. It had been a long day.

He listened for Tani and Joe, but the house was silent. Putting the cards back in his suitcase, Derek crawled onto the bed. He picked up the gold card his grandpa had given him and looked again at the picture of the whale. Derek turned the card over but it was blank. When he turned it back again, he thought he saw a face instead of the outline of the whale. It was there for only an instant, but he knew everything about it from just one look. The face belonged to a girl with shiny dark hair like his mother and his grandmother, and wide-set brown eyes like his own. She could have been his sister. He reached into the pocket of his suitcase for the picture of his mother. Didn't the girl look just like Wiba?

Derek shook his head. He was probably tired and seeing his own reflection in the shiny card. He wasn't sure what made him do it, but he stuck the card underneath his pillow. Then he lay down, trying to figure out what was bothering Tani.

He remembered that his mother got angry with his father once about killer whales. During dinner, his father had told Derek about the time he worked on a shrimp boat in Newport, Oregon. The fishermen watched the whales chase sea lions into the bay, circling them and closing in for the kill. They felt sorry for the sea lions when they heard their barks turn to squeals and saw the water turn red with blood.

"That's why they're called killer whales, you know," his dad had said. "Because they hunt in packs, like wolves."

They had both looked at his mother then. It was clear she was angry.

"*You* call them killer," she said. "I know them as black whales." Then she got up and walked out of the room. Derek's dad just shrugged and kept on eating.

The next day his mother brought it up again. "Human beings kill their food too, but we aren't called 'killer humans,' " she told Derek. "Black whales don't make their prey suffer. They are less like killers than we are sometimes." But Derek couldn't really see that it made any difference whether you called them killer whales or black whales or orcas.

Now he wondered if there wasn't some connection between the way his mother had reacted to his dad's story and the reason Tani seemed so angry about Ocean Park. He went to sleep, turning that over in his mind.

Derek didn't have any friends in Sutton County and there was no TV to watch (Joe had broken the tube putting it back in the set), but his grandparents kept him busy. First thing in the morning, he would help Tani weed her vegetable garden. Derek had never thought vegetables were anything to get excited about, but it was fun spotting his first pumpkin and zucchini when they appeared on the vines. The pumpkin looked like an orange tennis ball and the zucchini like a long, green finger.

Tani had given him an old set of gardening tools to use. She taught him how to work his way between the rows with his hoe, and how to turn over the soil to give the roots air and discourage the weeds.

Joe was always gone during those morning hours, riding his bike around town, visiting people "even older than he is," Tani said. Derek enjoyed spending time alone with Tani. He liked to watch her face as she held the first picked vegetable in her hand, studying it.

"This year I planted the cucumbers on the south side," she said one morning. "Roots too wet make it spongy inside." Derek nodded. He wasn't really sure what she meant, but he was pleased that she thought he did.

Joe was always home by lunchtime. "I got an alarm clock here in my stomach," he told Derek, wheeling up his old bike and leaning it against the garage. They ate on the screened-in porch at the back of the house. It was cool there. A fresh breeze blew through the room and Joe had put awnings over the windows to keep out the direct sun.

For lunch they always had cheese: Wisconsin jack, Swiss, and cheddar. There were thick slices of tomato to go along with it, applesauce, fresh-baked bread, and raspberry jelly.

Afterwards, he would go with his grandpa down to Roberts' Repair Shop, Joe leading the way on his bicycle and Derek following after him on his skateboard. One nice thing about Arcadia was that the town had good sidewalks. The cement was smooth and every once in a while a tree whose roots had grown big under the sidewalk made a miniature jump ramp. Derek liked to show his grandpa the tricks he had learned to do on his board.

Joe kept his repair shop even though he was retired and didn't fix farm machinery anymore. Now he collected old furniture, buggies, wagon wheels, organs— almost anything—and restored them. Of course, he also made the wooden toys that the church sold at its Christmas bazaar.

By the third week, Joe thought Derek was familiar enough with the equipment to start making a wooden train. Even though he was too big for one himself and he didn't really know any little kids, Derek was excited at the idea of building something with his hands.

"Why don't we start with a boxcar, then move up to the engine?" Joe suggested.

As he showed Derek how to trace the pattern onto

the wood, he asked, "You ever going to use that card I gave you?"

"I want to. It's just . . ."

"You don't have to worry so much about your grandma, you know," Joe said, pressing gently on Derek's hand so the tracing pencil would make a darker line. "She has some different ideas about things. You can respect a person's ideas without agreeing with them." Joe used his fingernail to etch the line into the soft wood. "Are you following me?"

Derek wasn't sure if Joe meant what he was doing with the pattern or what he was saying. "Not really."

"Well, because of the way she grew up, Tani looks at things a little differently than you and me." Joe took the slab of wood with the pattern traced on it over to the circle saw and clamped it down. "That's okay. But if you want to go to Ocean Park, she'll understand."

When Joe said "the way she grew up," Derek knew he was referring to his grandmother's Indian upbringing. He wondered what Tani had thought about killer whales as a child. Growing up in the Queen Charlotte Islands off British Columbia, she must have seen them. He wanted to know more, but then Joe asked him to help brace the wood, and Derek decided he would just have to wait.

"Well, when can I go?"

"Soon as you want. How's tomorrow sound?"

"Sounds great," Derek said, and the subject was dropped.

The next morning, after Derek helped Tani stake the snap beans and mulch the cucumbers, he and Joe washed up and left for Ocean Park. If she was upset about it, Tani wasn't letting on. She even made a picnic lunch for them.

"Don't eat too much junk," she said, handing them a heavy sack. "It's not good for you."

"Don't worry so much," Joe told her after he'd given her a kiss and a hug. "It's not good for you."

Four

The Dolphin Girl

To get to Ocean Park, Derek and Joe drove to the outskirts of town and past wide, patchwork swathes of corn and wheat.

"We haven't had much rain this year," Joe said, inspecting the crops. "The corn should be a few inches taller than it is now." Derek rolled his window down to drink in the fresh morning air. "But at least we have a cool morning."

It didn't seem that cool to Derek, but then he was used to the cool weather. It made him think of early mornings in Port Espadon, when he'd walk down to the docks to see his dad off for a day of fishing. Derek put his hand out the window and let the strong wind skim over his palm.

They followed the signs to Ocean Park and finally

turned down a broad avenue lined with potted palms.
To their right, Derek and Joe saw several parking lots,
all of them nearly empty. They parked in the closest
one and followed a path to the park entrance.

WELCOME TO OCEAN PARK read a glistening fiberglass
sign above the ticket booths. Underneath the words
was a life-sized carving of a killer whale, its open mouth
formed into a big toothy grin as it looked down over the
small clusters of park guests. Joe and Derek flashed
their gold cards and the man in the ticket booth smiled.

"Gold card members are always welcome." He
clicked his attendance counter twice.

Once inside the gate, Derek felt as if he had
entered a different world. A moment ago, they had
been in a parking lot in the middle of Sutton County.
Now, flowering bushes, trees, and plants were everywhere, their scents heavy in the surrounding mist.
Steam rose from the asphalt paths, floating through the
branches of tree ferns and palm fronds. Exotic birds sat
calmly preening their feathers on tall bamboo perches.
In the distance, Derek could hear the barking of sea
lions. Without thinking, he started toward the noise,
but Joe caught his arm.

"Didn't I tell you this place was amazing?" He pulled
Derek over to a wrought-iron bench and spread out a
park map on their laps. "The sea lions are part of the

pinniped exhibit." Derek watched Joe trace his finger over the worn map. "If we follow this path, we can see them and the dolphins before the first whale show."

"You miss the ocean too sometimes, don't you, Joe?"

"More than I'd admit to the woman I dragged away from it." Joe patted the breast pocket of his work shirt and fished out a stub of pencil.

"Why did you come here?" Derek knew that Joe and Tani had met while Joe was a surveyor in a logging camp in Canada. She had been with her tribe then and her father didn't want her to marry Joe.

"When the Depression hit, Uncle Sam offered me a job here and I wasn't in a position to say no."

"Did Tani want to come here?"

"She never said much about it. Her father wanted her to marry a Haida, and her brother Kwung was raising hell with the white fishermen and just about anyone else he could pick a fight with." Joe made check marks next to certain locations on the map. Then he carefully folded it and put both the pencil and map away.

"I'll tell you one thing. That woman was born with one foot in the water, and it was a damn shame that I took her away from it." Joe looked out over Derek's head. "But at the time, I thought I had no choice."

Both Derek and Joe were silent for a while, watching a tall figure in a whale costume greeting children. The whale would put his fin around a child and some adult would snap a picture. The head of the costume had a big grin, with a huge pink tongue hanging between the parted teeth.

Remembering his dad's story about the poor sea lions, Derek said to Joe, "They sure make killer whales look friendly."

Derek squinted at the whale's mouth to see the face hidden inside as the costumed character made its way over to them and sat down next to Joe.

"One of you guys want my job?" he asked. "The pay's lousy, and it's twenty degrees hotter in here, but as long as you don't mind little kids spilling ice cream all over you, you'll do just fine."

"Clem?" Joe pushed the whale's tongue aside to get a clearer view of the speaker.

"None other." Clem stuck out a fin and Derek shook it.

"What are you doing in there?" Joe asked, laughing. "You really need money that bad?"

"Nah. But the kids pretty much run the dairy now. I can't hang around all summer watching them screw it up, you know." Clem stroked his tongue thoughtfully. "Better get back to work. Katy the Whale isn't supposed to sit down on the job."

Derek and Joe watched Clem wander off, waving to the crowds.

"I'll be darned," Joe said, laughing at the funny figure. "Old Clem in a whale costume." He watched Clem for a moment before leading Derek in the direction of the barking sea lions.

Derek was no stranger to sea lion antics. Whenever he went down to the docks in Port Espadon, he would see them rolling in the water and begging. The fishermen would clean their catches at tables built on the piers and then wash the entrails overboard, providing the sea lions with a free meal.

The pinniped exhibit consisted of a large pool with an artificial rock rising out of the center. Perched on the rock was an elephant seal, his long snout like an elephant's trunk. In the background, Derek could see that they had tried to imitate the rocky shore of the ocean. On one of the few smooth surfaces, a couple of big sea lions were entertaining the small crowd by barking at each other and fighting for position. Harbor seals peered shyly at the humans from the water.

A girl in uniform stood at a little podium on the right side of the enclosure. She had a green cardigan on over a blue-spangled top and a pair of shorts. Derek noticed that she had goose bumps on her legs and kept her arms wrapped tightly around her as she talked about the exhibit. The name *Ann* was printed on her name tag.

"Why doesn't she just wear pants?" Derek whispered to Joe.

"It's supposed to be part of the appeal, I think," Joe answered, patting Derek's hand.

"Oh."

"It may be too cold for me," Ann was saying, "but they love it." She nodded toward the sea lions, who seemed in a playful mood. "With all this heat, they've been pretty sleepy lately."

Derek went to the edge of the enclosure and looked down. A harbor seal poked its whiskered nose out of the water and looked up at him.

"Hello, you," Derek said softly to the familiar face. "I've seen you before." The harbor seal seemed to understand the greeting because he dove underwater, waving his small tail flippers in the air.

After a few minutes, Joe said, "We can catch the next whale show if we hurry. Let's go."

"Can't we just go by the dolphin-petting pool? I've never seen dolphins in person." Joe nodded and they crossed a bridge with brightly colored fish swimming in the stream below it. On the other side, a row of vendors were selling lemonade, flowers, and toy marine animals. Joe and Derek paused to watch a mime pretending to pull bills from her pocket to pay for a bunch of flowers.

Up ahead there was some commotion. A little boy about eight years old was sitting on the ground, in the middle of an enormous puddle, crying. The boy was soaked from head to toe.

A teenager in a blue park uniform was trying to clean up what seemed like half the pool's water. He mopped right around the little boy while the child's mother tried to comfort him and still stay dry. Though Derek couldn't get very close, he could make out the deep gray backs of several dolphins. They seemed to have formed a tight circle and were moving very fast around the pool, rising to breathe together.

Finally, they broke apart and Derek sloshed through some of the water to the teenager with the mop and tugged on his shirt.

"Do they do that often?"

The park attendant looked at Derek, then glanced over at the pool. "What? Swim like that?" He squeezed the water into a large pail. "Nope. Only after *she's* been here."

"Who's she?" was, of course, the next logical question. Derek was about to ask it when he saw an electric golf cart approaching. The young man with the mop started working three times as fast, sloshing water in all directions so that it lapped up against the little boy's legs, making him cry even harder.

"Stop bugging me and let me do my work, okay?" the attendant said to Derek, glancing around nervously.

In a minute the golf cart had rounded the corner and another boy with a mop jumped off the back and ran up to the first one.

The driver, a tall, slim man with a deep tan, carefully adjusted his baseball cap and said something into a walkie-talkie. He placed it back in the holster at his side and then approached the two park attendants. He pulled the first one aside and spoke in that low, controlled adult voice that Derek knew always meant trouble.

"Can you tell me what happened here, Jerry?"

"Hello, Mr. Beaman, sir. Well, okay. I was stocking the cooler with fish when I looked up and saw this kid here." He motioned toward the little boy, who had managed to stop crying but still hiccupped now and then. "He was poking at the dolphins with one of those swords they sell over in Bluebeard's Gift Shop. But then the kid told me that *she* appeared . . . described her just like the others did. . . ."

"Wait a minute. *Who* saw *what?*"

"You know . . ." Jerry looked around nervously, as if

he couldn't afford to be overheard. Then he whispered, "*She* saw the kid here poking the dolphin."

Mr. Beaman understood then. Slowly, he took off his baseball cap and wiped the sweat from his forehead before fitting it back on. "And then?"

"Well . . . there was this noise like something heavy hitting the water and then a splash so big it knocked the little kid right on his bottom." The strange thing was, Derek noticed, the pool was full. "All right, folks, that's it," said Mr. Beaman, taking charge. He waved his arms at Joe and Derek and the few others who were milling around. "Let us get this cleaned up, please." He turned and spoke to the woman, who was still bending over her little boy, trying to wring out the tail end of his shirt. "If you'll come with me, ma'am, I think we'll be able to take care of your son and get him some dry clothes." Mr. Beaman deposited the soaking wet child in the back of his electric cart and helped the boy's mother into the passenger's seat.

"Timmy says he saw a witch with a great big cape and hat," his mother was saying as the golf cart drove away. "Does she play a part in one of your shows?"

The crowd seemed to feel the excitement was over, and most of them went off in the direction of the whale stadium. Joe wanted to go too, but Derek still wasn't ready. He was hoping the two boys would talk about what had happened and then he would find out who this mysterious "she" was. He was right.

"The dolphin girl again?" the second boy said to Jerry in a low voice Derek could barely hear.

"Yeah, and it serves that kid right, too."

"Have you ever seen her?"

"I don't know. Sometimes I think I see something faint for a second, like an outline of a girl. But I don't think she's a witch, Glenn."

"What is she then?" Glenn asked as their mops met over the pail.

"I don't know, but she gives me the creeps." Jerry took the pail and dumped the water onto a hydrangea bush.

"That's salt water, you idiot." Glenn knocked Jerry with the handle of his mop. "That old gardener is going to have your head."

"C'mon, Derek," said Joe, starting off in the direction of the whale stadium.

"I'll be right there." Something drew him over to the pool. Derek leaned over the edge and put his hands in the water.

The dolphins swam lazily around the pool, rising up to chatter at him. Derek realized that whatever mystery had been there for him to discover was gone.

He watched the dolphins swim over one another in

the small pool and wondered what they thought about all day, how they entertained themselves. Did they enjoy looking at people?

He turned to Jerry and said, "Can you tell me where these dolphins came from?"

"What?"

"Where did you catch the dolphins?" Jerry and Glenn exchanged a look. "We don't catch them," Jerry said. "We collect them."

"What's the difference?"

"You boys can talk about this later," Joe said. "After the whale show."

They climbed up a long hill to the whale stadium, entering from the back. Joe paused to rest a minute, leaning against a small office door marked SOUND BOOTH. Derek walked around to the front, and through the window he saw all kinds of equipment, including a panel of dials and switches. Joe explained that from this little booth, an operator could control the music and lights, and could make sure that the actors were heard throughout the stadium.

They took seats about halfway to the stage. A group of children, all five or six years old, were lined up in the first row along the edge of the tank wall. A sign near the front of the stadium read CAUTION: FIRST TEN ROWS ARE A WATER ZONE. A few elderly couples sat here and there, but the stadium was mostly empty, which made it seem even bigger.

It was covered but it had no walls, which made Derek feel that he was inside and outside at the same time. In front of the stage, a large tank of water was sunk deep into the ground. The side closest to the audience formed a semicircle. A clear wall surrounded this half, so that Derek could see both above and below the water. The other side of the tank met with the stage and a slide-out platform, which disappeared into the crystal blue water the way sand does into the ocean.

The only way to reach the stage, unless you swam there, was through a doorway at the back. On either side of the main stage but partially hidden behind the large tank of water were two smaller tanks. The backdrop was decorated with red, white, and blue streamers. From the ceiling hung a banner that read KATY GOES TO ENGLAND.

Suddenly a huge black-and-white shape appeared underwater. The whale seemed a little out of focus, the way things do when seen underwater, but still giant and powerful. Just as quickly, it disappeared again. Derek could tell that it was swimming between the two pools.

"Good afternoon, ladies and gentlemen." A man's voice with an English accent came over the loudspeaker. Then he stepped onto the stage, dressed in an army uniform covered with medals. A sword was strapped to his side. "Welcome to Ocean Park and today's presentation of 'Katy Goes To England.' " As he said this, he raised his arm and saluted a large portrait of the queen that hung just above and to the side of the pool. Then he turned back to the audience.

"We know how much you love Katy in America," he said. "So, the queen asked the president of the United States to appoint Katy ambassador to England. Today, she arrives at Buckingham Palace." He paused, putting his hand to his ear and leaning toward the stage entrance. "Here's the queen now."

Music came over the loudspeakers and the man on stage put his hand over his heart and began singing *God Save the Queen.* A woman stepped out on stage. Her hair was piled on top of her head and surrounded by a sparkling crown. A deep purple robe trimmed in fur covered her entire body. Only her hands, holding a long golden scepter with a glass crystal at the end, were visible.

She stepped up close to the man, who was busy singing and making funny faces at the audience, and rapped him over the head with her scepter.

"That's enough, Reginald," she scolded. The audience broke into laughter.

"Yes, Your Highness." Reginald bowed deeply.

"Well, where's the new ambassador from the United States?" she asked, looking around, her nose high in the air. "I don't like to be kept waiting, Reginald." She had turned away and was pulling off her long gloves when Derek saw the large black-and-white shape appear again under the water.

Then, so suddenly it made the whole audience gasp, the whale slid out onto the platform, opening her mouth wide, just inches from the queen's back. Reginald inched backward.

"Uh, Your Highness?" he said.

"When I attended queen preparatory school, I was taught time and again that the queen waits for *no* man. Well, in this case, no *whale*." At that, she turned around and screamed, dropping her scepter into the water. Derek was afraid she was going to faint dead away. But what she did was just as surprising. The queen shouted, "Katy, you're here!" then stuck her arm into the whale's mouth and began rubbing her large pink tongue. Reginald took a handkerchief from his breast pocket and wiped his brow.

When she finished, she stood up and said, "Do be a dear and fetch my scepter, Katy. As you know, the queen doesn't swim." Katy worked her way off the platform and back into the water. She took the scepter in her mouth and swam back to the queen. Then she raised herself out of the water just enough to be at arm's level with the queen, who took the scepter, wiped it off on her robe, and used it to knock Reginald over the head again. The audience laughed again, even louder this time. Several people clapped.

"Be a dear, Reginald, and serve tea." Reginald disappeared, rubbing the top of his head. The queen turned again to Katy.

"Now, tell me, dear. What have you been up to in America?" She put her hand to her ear as the whale rose out of the water, opening and closing her great mouth. "Working at Ocean Park, you say?" The queen sighed and readjusted her crown. "I always thought working would be such a hard way to make a living." She leaned back toward the whale again to listen.

"That easy? Good heavens. What is it that you do?" Then she stood back and gave a short wave with her hand. Suddenly, she was no longer a silly queen. Derek realized she was giving the whale a signal. Katy disappeared under the water and began racing around the edge of the pool. Everyone in the audience seemed to sit up straighter, waiting to see how Katy was going to turn all that power into a stunt. Then, as if it had already happened, as if she had already done the fantastic trick everyone was waiting for, she stopped moving and floated to the top of the pool.

Derek looked at Joe, disappointed. "Did I miss it?" he asked.

"No, I don't think so." Joe seemed confused, too. "I'm pretty sure this is the part where Katy sloshes water on the audience." One look at the queen and Derek could tell something was wrong. Her back was turned to them and she kept pressing a button at the side of the pool.

"Reginald," she shouted, "I think you might bring that tea *now*." Then she turned to the audience and said, "I've always heard that it's hard to work on an empty stomach." All the while, Katy floated listlessly on the surface. Reginald came out with a tray in one hand and a large pail of fish in the other. The queen grabbed a fish and threw it into the water so that it landed just beyond Katy's mouth. Then she went to the side of the pool and pressed the button again.

"What's the button for?" Derek asked, leaning close to Joe.

It wasn't Joe who answered. "It makes a high-pitched noise under the water," said a voice directly behind him. "She uses it to give me directions or to reward me when I've done a trick well. Right now, she's just trying to get a response."

He turned and saw her, the girl from the front of

his card who looked so much like his mother as a girl. She was dressed in a pair of jeans and a tie-dyed T-shirt.

Still eyeing the motionless whale in the pool, Joe finally answered. "I'm not sure," he said, as though he hadn't heard the girl behind them at all.

"She just told us," Derek said to Joe, pointing over his shoulder. "It's a signal."

"What? Who just told us?"

"He can't see or hear me," the girl told Derek. "Because he doesn't believe I can exist."

Derek looked at her, puzzled. How could Joe not believe his own eyes? The girl was sitting right there, yet it was true. Joe couldn't see her.

"Why won't the whale perform this trick?" he asked her.

"Derek. Who are you talking to?" Joe was straining to see behind him.

"Why should she?" said the girl, who seemed a bit irritated by the question. Then she smiled mysteriously. "She's already performed it once today."

Derek shifted back around in his seat. "I'd just like to see the trick, that's all," he said.

"You almost did." Her voice was right next to his ear this time, her breath cool as it passed his face. "I'll give you a second chance."

When he turned around again to look for her, she was gone.

The audience tried not to look at the stage. It was like looking straight at someone who is making a speech but has lost her place. And the audience could see it was no easy task convincing a two-ton, twenty-foot creature to do *anything* it didn't want to do.

"I'm afraid that Katy is a little tired today," said the queen, dropping her British accent and addressing the audience directly. "Sometimes she . . ." But at this moment the whale dove, rising once to collect the fish that lay on the surface. Just as quickly, the queen stood back, looking once again like someone in charge, giving directions with short waves of her hand. For the second time, Katy raced around the pool and the audience strained to get a better view. Then her smooth body cut out of the water until just her tail fins touched the surface, and she made herself flat, so that all of her would hit the water at the same time.

As soon as the children in the front row realized what was about to happen, they covered their heads and squealed with delight. Katy crashed back into the pool, displacing hundreds of gallons of water and soaking the audience in the first ten rows.

"That's very interesting," said the queen, when Katy had doused the audience on every side of the pool and returned to the stage where she was standing. "I could use that trick when I'm arguing before Parliament. Shall we have tea?" Katy nodded her head vigorously to indicate yes. The queen took two fish out of the pail and threw them to Katy. When Katy had swallowed them, she swam onto the slide-out platform. The queen brought over a big teapot, obviously filled with water, and began pouring it into the whale's open mouth, which, Derek noticed, was nearly six feet across and filled with sturdy, round teeth.

"Do you take sugar?" asked the queen. Again Katy nodded yes, and the queen took two small cubes and placed them far inside the whale's mouth on her tongue. Then she rubbed the whale's tongue vigorously. Katy wagged her tail fins up and down and the whole audience laughed and applauded.

"Now if I could only find my cup, we'd be right as rain." But as the queen turned around, she lost her footing on the slippery platform and sank into the water. Suddenly, all that was left of her was the purple circle of her robe and her crown floating just in the middle where her head should have been.

Reginald got down on his hands and knees and grabbed the robe and crown from the water. "Oh, dear! Oh, my! The king will have my head for this. Katy," he cried, "you've got to save me! I mean her. I mean Her

Highness. The queen can't swim!" Katy seemed to understand and she worked her way off the platform and disappeared under the water. At the same time, the queen appeared on the surface, sputtering and gasping.

Just as the queen seemed to be losing the last of her strength, Katy's broad back buoyed her up. The audience could see that underneath her cloak, she had been wearing a bathing suit all along. She held onto Katy's dorsal fin and rode her around the pool. When the queen had recovered herself a bit, she stood up, waving to the audience the way queens do whenever there are subjects around. As she passed Reginald, who was busy wringing his hands, she said, "Reginald. This is charming. You must try it."

"Please come out of the water now, Your Highness. You might catch your death of cold."

"No," she said, turning her back to him and crossing her arms. "I'd rather stay out here and play with Katy." With that, she sat down again and straddled the whale, grabbing hold of her pectoral fins. Katy dove again and surfaced, leaping into the air with the queen on her back. The audience went wild with applause.

"She must be awfully brave," Joe said. "If she fell off, that whale could crush her."

"That whale wouldn't hurt her," Derek said, feeling

as if he knew it for a fact. "Look how careful Katy is with her."

They watched as the queen and Katy performed several more tricks together. Katy rolled in the water with the queen on her back. The queen placed both feet on Katy's pectoral fins and put her arms around the top of Katy's head. When Katy leaped out of the water and flopped onto her back, the queen sailed overhead, diving into the water several feet away. Finally, Katy swam over to the platform and the queen jumped back onto the stage, to the delight of Reginald.

"Must you go so soon?" the queen asked. When Katy nodded yes, the queen made a big circle with her hands. Katy came out of the water just long enough to give her a big, wet kiss. Reginald looked astonished.

"No one kisses the queen," he said.

"I've always had trouble with that rule," the queen said, rubbing her chin. Then she turned and kissed Reginald. They both waved good-bye to Katy, who had rolled onto her side and was waving a pectoral fin back at them as she swam into the other pool. Over the loudspeaker, a voice said: "Let's have a big round of applause for Rick Lane, as Reginald, Theresa Summers, as the queen, and Katy, as Katy, the killer whale."

The audience gave them a standing ovation.

Five

Smart But Not Wise

As soon as they reached the house, Derek went to his room. He grabbed his baseball cards from the bottom dresser drawer and sat back on the bed. One by one, he flipped the cards toward the wastebasket, something he often did when he was thinking. And he had a lot to think about.

Was the girl he spoke with the same one who had caused the huge wave at the dolphin pool? Why hadn't Joe seen her? Derek was sure it was her face he'd seen on his gold card.

He wondered if she looked nice to him because she was pretty or because she reminded him so much of his mother. Glancing down at the baseball card in his hand, Derek saw her face again, instead of Jim Palmer's. It was too much. He threw the card down on the bed, jumped to the floor, and ran downstairs.

"Joe's gone to his workshop," Tani said as Derek came into the kitchen. "He thought maybe you were sleeping, so he went alone."

"That's okay." Actually, Derek was relieved. He didn't want to be around Joe just now. They'd talked about what happened on the way home and it was clear to him that Joe didn't believe a word he said.

"Can I call my mom, Tani?" Tani nodded and told Derek to go into the den where he'd have more privacy. Derek ran down the hall and closed the den door harder than he meant to.

"Derek?" His mom sounded surprised to hear from him since this wasn't Sunday night, when they usually talked. "Is something wrong, honey?"

Derek felt comforted by the sound of her voice, but now that he had her on the phone he wasn't sure what he wanted to say.

"I've got something to tell you." There was a pause while she waited. "I took some of your baseball cards with me. I busted up your '74 Expos, White Sox, and Cubs sets." There was another long pause. "I'm sorry."

"You could have just asked me."

"I know." After they'd hung up, Derek sat in the den for a long time, tapping at the keys of his grandfather's ancient typewriter. He'd wanted to tell his mom all about the girl, but it was hard to talk about something like that over the phone. It occurred to him that one of the reasons his mom and dad had broken up was because his dad was away on the fishing boats for so long. Derek had only been away from her a month, but already he couldn't really remember the things about her that seemed most important. Like the way she messed with his hair, for instance. Or how warm and dry her hands always felt.

Back in the kitchen, Tani sat shelling peas into a chipped enamel strainer wedged between her legs. Derek listened to the peas plink against the bottom as she tore open each pod.

Tani asked him to go pick some Swiss chard from the garden. When he got back, she gave him a bowl of his own and he began tearing the tough center rib from each leaf.

"You have a good time at that ocean place?" she asked when they were both settled.

"Yeah." Derek found a caterpillar on one of the leaves, tapped it into his palm, then set it outside the back door.

"It make you feel at home?"

"Oh, no." He stopped for a minute. He didn't want to hurt Tani's feelings. "I feel kind of bad for the people here. They can see a dolphin, but not the way I've seen porpoises. It's not nearly as nice as watching them race a fishing boat or play with each other in the ocean." He wanted to explain it more, but Tani was bent over her bowl, frowning, her quick brown hands making short work of the peas.

"It's not that I didn't have a good time," Derek added. "The whale was amazing."

Tani set the peas on the kitchen table, then wiped her hands on her skirt. She settled back, folding her hands in her lap and crossing her legs at her ankles.

"Joe tells me you heard a voice. I want to hear about that."

So Derek told her. About the card and the dolphins and the girl at the stadium. He told her just the way he'd wanted to tell his mom. And he didn't feel stupid, either, because the way Tani was nodding her head and looking so thoughtful, he knew she believed him.

When he was done, she said, "As far as I can figure it, that whale wants something from you."

"What?"

Tani got up from her chair. "Maybe I should go back a ways." She got up and rummaged through the cupboards for a big pot. Dumping in the peas, she added a few cupfuls of water, while Derek waited impatiently. When Tani had something really important to say, she could act like there was no rush at all. Finally, after the pot began hissing, she returned to sit with him again.

"The Haida believe that animals can take the form of humans. But they do so because they want something. If this whale is appearing to you as a girl. . . ."

"But what could she want, Tani?"

Tani shrugged. "I guess she'll tell you when you're ready."

"I don't know," Derek said.

"You must know a little," Tani smiled, patting his knee. "Or else you wouldn't be able to see her." She got up and poured them both a glass of lemonade. Then they went to sit out on the back porch step, where the fireflies were just beginning to light up the dusky sky.

"Your mother," Tani told Derek slowly, "knows very little about Haida ways. To be honest, I decided long ago not to teach her. But lately, I'm beginning to think I was wrong."

Derek waited for her to go on. After several minutes, she said, "Once, there were many Haida living on the Queen Charlotte Islands. Well, that's not what we called the islands. We called them Haida Gwaii, Land-of-Our-People. In the summertime, our people went to fishing villages and hunted salmon and halibut and cod and herring. We took sea lions and otters for their warm skins and gathered crab apples and wild berries.

We never harmed the black whale, though, the one they now call killer. We called black whales the People-Who-Live-in-the-Land-Below-the-Sea. We believed the black whales lived just like us, had families, had celebrations.

"By the time my mother was born, the old ways had already changed. Traders had set up posts on our island. The whaling companies had drawn many of our young men to their ships. Her family found it harder and harder to find enough fish and enough skins, because so many had taken so much.

"So, when she was still a young girl, many Haida paddled far away, to Victoria, to find work. But they were sent back to their island because there was a horrible sickness going around the city. It was the smallpox." Tani sat quietly for a moment before getting up from the step. Derek watched her through the doorway as she stirred the peas with a long wooden spoon, drained them in the sink, and poured them into a bowl. She dotted them with butter, and set the bowl in the oven.

"There was no cure then," she continued, after she had returned to her seat. "Some of the Haida people caught the sickness in Victoria, and they brought the disease back and infected our people. Soon, there were almost no Haida left. Before the sickness, the Haida people wanted nothing to do with the missionaries who came and tried to convert them. We were proud of our way of life and did not wish to change it. But after so many died, the missionaries came again and we took their Christian names. We went to their schools and learned their English. Few of our customs survived.

"Though I grew up at Masset, all I can remember are the towering crest poles, gray with age and covered with vines and moss. And the stories I was told." Tani sighed, and drank the rest of her lemonade before setting her glass down on the step.

Derek didn't know what to say. Tani had finally told him something about her past, but what did it mean?

"Joe thinks he took me away from my home, the ocean," she said. "I know it would have been worse to stay among the ghosts." She looked hard at Derek. "But if what you're telling me is true, then our ways haven't died. You owe it yourself and to this black whale to find out what she wants." Tani got up then and left Derek by himself on the back step. She returned and handed him a small object wrapped in white cloth.

"Maybe this can help you," she said. Derek unwrapped the object. It was a carving of a black whale. At first, Derek thought it was carved from wood, but the material was too hard and shiny black to be wood.

Flowing lines and intricate circles within circles covered the whale's back. A large set of teeth and a powerful tail made it look almost frightening.

"This is a carving from argillite, a soft black stone that is mined only from quarries on the Haida Gwaii. My mother belonged to the Black Whale Clan. She gave this to me. Carry it with you and maybe it will help you understand."

They saw the wavering headlight of Joe's bicycle coming up the drive. Tani took the whale from Derek and wrapped it carefully back in the white cloth. Then she hid it in her apron and put a finger to her lips. Joe came up the walk, wiping his forehead on his sleeve.

"I think I've got it all figured out. It's this dry weather. You sweat so fast you don't realize how much water you're losing." He fished an ice cube out of Tani's glass and sucked on it.

"You can start seeing things when you're dehydrated, you know."

Derek looked first at Tani, then back at Joe. "Maybe you're right," he told his grandfather.

After Joe went to wash up for dinner, Tani said, "The Haida have a saying that 'the world is as sharp as a knife,' Derek. It means not to expect anything and to expect everything. Be careful." Derek wanted to ask her to explain it further, but Joe came out of the bathroom, rubbing his hands together and shouting, "Now, what's for dinner?"

The next day, Derek helped his grandfather pick the first raspberries of the season. Picking raspberries was slow work. He had to search carefully under the leaves for the hidden fruit. Derek had a lot of time to think while he was filling up the quart baskets. What could a whale want from him?

The night before, Tani had suggested he think like the whale to find out what the whale wanted. Now he tried, if for no other reason than to keep his mind off the thick heat and the black flies.

Tani had told him that the difference between her and Joe was that she grew up believing that black whales had great powers and Joe didn't. That's why she knew Derek was telling the truth. But Derek still didn't know if *he* believed the whale had great powers. When he looked at the evidence, all he'd seen was a big puddle and a girl who looked like his mom. And all he'd heard was a voice his grandpa couldn't hear. Was that really so out of the ordinary? But somehow, Derek knew that to dismiss it all would be too easy.

Derek had asked Tani to go with him to Ocean Park, to help him figure out the puzzle, but she refused. "The whale girl doesn't want to talk to me. It's you she wants."

Even Joe wasn't ready to go back yet. "I'll just drop you off, if that's okay," he said on the first morning Derek could go. "I've got an Antique Wheelers meeting this morning and then I've got to inspect the fairground this afternoon."

As much as Tani loved to tease Joe for being a lazy old man, Derek had never met anyone as busy as his grandfather. The Antique Wheelers showed off their vintage cars at county fairs all over Wisconsin. And Joe was in charge of the whole Sutton County Fair this year. Just thinking about his grandparents made Derek smile. And he knew they were right: today he should go to Ocean Park alone.

Once he entered the park, Derek wasn't sure what to do. It was too early for any shows. In fact, he was one of the first visitors. He made his way slowly toward the whale stadium. At first, Derek thought he might look at the aquarium or the beluga whale or the walruses, exhibits he and Joe had missed the last time. But when he came to the path that would take him to that side of the park, he lost interest. He felt drawn to the whale stadium to see the black whale (Tani wouldn't let him say "killer whale" anymore) up close.

The whale wasn't in the one of the smaller display tanks, which meant she had to be in the main show pool. Derek could hear the soft whoosh of her breathing. There was a chain across the stadium entrance and a sign that read WHALE STADIUM CLOSED. NEXT SHOW AT 11:00. Derek slipped under it and walked up to the glass. Beneath the water, he could see the long sleek body of the black whale. Her white markings were so neat and graceful that she looked as if she had been painted by an artist. Using short flicks of her powerful tail, she swam against the far side of the tank, by the trainer's platform. When she opened her mouth, Derek saw the rows of round white teeth that looked as if they could grind up just about anything. Without thinking, he touched the whale carving in his pocket. He had studied it so long in his room that the teeth no longer seemed menacing. But seeing the real thing up close made him glad she belonged in the water while he belonged on land.

In the distance, Derek heard music. He wasn't sure just what kind. The notes were high and soft. Only one instrument was being played. The whale must have heard the music too, because she lifted her head out of the water and swam over to where the sounds were coming from. Did whales like music? He would have to ask the whale girl when he saw her again.

If he saw her again. Derek still had a hard time believing in whales who could turn into girls who could turn into whales.

He heard noises and ducked down. Then he realized that as long as he stayed close to the tank, no one from the platform could see him.

Rick and Theresa, the trainers from yesterday's whale show, walked onto the stage.

"I wish I weren't leaving so soon," Rick said.

"Well, I'm glad we're through with the English routine. I've always thought it was too slapstick."

"From what I've seen," Rick went on, "you seem to have everything under control with the new show. Has your costume arrived?"

"What costume? I'm supposed to wear a white tank suit."

"That's not what I heard. Headquarters says lots of sequins on a bathing suit that's cut high and low."

"Well, then," Theresa said, "they can send somebody new to put into it. I'm wearing a tank suit." They stopped talking and, for a few minutes, Derek heard only the sound of props being moved around on the stage.

"You know," Theresa said finally, "I'm getting tired of them treating us like we're a circus act. We're trained professionals, aren't we, Katy?" Derek watched the whale, half expecting her to rise up and nod her head yes.

"I don't know, Theresa. I think you'd look good in that costume. I'd like to see you in it, anyway." Suddenly Derek felt embarrassed about his eavesdropping. Theresa laughed.

"I'll see you tonight," she said. Derek heard the stage door open and close. There was another long silence. When he thought it was safe to look at the stage, Derek saw Theresa carrying a pail of fish toward the pool.

"Look, Katy, I got salmon." Theresa was wearing a blue jogging suit and had her hair tied up in a ponytail. She threw a few fish into the whale's mouth.

"Rick says you should only have this as a reward for practicing the new routine. But we don't really care what Rick thinks, do we?" Theresa's hand disappeared inside Katy's mouth. Then she sat back.

"Don't I even get a thank-you?" she said. "Say 'thank you, Theresa.'" Instead of saying thank you, Katy used her powerful tail to push her body halfway out of the water. She extended a pectoral fin to Theresa.

"I guess a handshake's as good as a thank-you," Theresa said, laughing. She stood back and took off her jogging suit. Underneath, she had on a swimsuit. Derek was amazed at how muscular she was. He had never seen a woman with such strong-looking arms and legs. She dove into the water. Now Derek was sure that he would be seen, but neither the woman nor the whale seemed interested in anything but what they were doing.

Theresa took hold of Katy's dorsal fin and slowly the whale turned over and over, stopping on her back. Theresa climbed onto Katy's white belly and balanced on her hands while Katy skimmed through the water. Then they both dove. When they surfaced, Theresa was sitting on one of Katy's pectoral fins. It was like a ballet that Derek had seen on TV once, where the man lifted the woman up and balanced her on his shoulder. If Derek hadn't known better, he'd say they were dancing.

The whale and the woman fell back into the water. When Theresa surfaced, Derek could see that she was pleased. He decided to leave then, while they were still busy. He started making his way quietly to the side entrance.

"That was great," she yelled, climbing onto Katy's underside and rubbing the area beneath her pectoral fins. "We've got the first half of the program down pat. The directors won't know what hit them at the preview tomorrow. You've never been . . ." Suddenly, Katy twisted around, dumping Theresa in the water. Derek knew then that the whale had sensed him and he froze.

"Katy?" Theresa was pulling herself up on the platform. In an instant, Katy was at Derek's side of the pool, leaping and diving in the tight confines of the tank.

"Is someone there?" Theresa shouted. "This is a private session." Derek ducked down and ran, clearing the chain at the entrance with about a foot to spare.

"Hey! Come back here, kid!" was the last thing he heard, and he didn't stop running until he reached the other end of the park.

Derek sat down on a bench to catch his breath. He remembered what Joe had said about seeing things, and decided to get something to drink. As he looked for a refreshment stand, Derek wondered if Katy would ask her trainer, Theresa, if she wanted something. She seemed like a nice lady. Derek pulled the whale carving out of his pocket and rubbed his finger across its shiny back.

"When do you start giving me the answers?" he asked softly. He spotted a lemonade stand not far away and reached farther down in his pocket for some money.

The girl behind the counter poured a glass of freshly made lemonade into a large cup.

"That'll be eighty cents, please." Derek handed her a dollar.

"Nickels okay?" she asked. "I'm low on dimes."

"Sure," Derek said. He reached for the coins, but another hand shot out from behind him and grabbed the change.

"Hey!" Derek turned around to face the thief. It was her. Except for the long hair, Derek might have been looking in a mirror. He forgot about the money and backed away, sloshing lemonade all over his shirt.

"Can I taste it?" she asked.

Derek tried to speak. He knew he should at least give her a sip. But somehow he couldn't. "Are you a whale?" he asked, feeling ridiculous as soon as he said it.

"You've been talking with your grandmother, haven't you?" she said, acting as if his question was perfectly normal.

"How do you know about my grandmother?"

"I know about a lot of things." Derek remembered her request and handed her the cup. She took a small sip, pressed her lips together, then started coughing. Derek patted her on the back.

"Katy? Are you all right?" As soon as he said the name, she straightened and looked away, staring at something in the opposite direction. Then she blinked a few times and looked back.

"That is not my name," she said firmly. They started walking, not because there was anywhere special to go but because Derek felt more comfortable moving than standing still.

"Well, who are you then?"

"It is less important for you to know who I am than to remember who *you* are," she said.

"I know who I am," Derek said. "I'm Der . . ."

Suddenly, she grabbed his hand, led him over to a grassy slope, and sat down by a sign that read PLEASE KEEP OFF THE GRASS.

"Uh, we're not supposed to sit here."

"Why not?"

Derek pointed to the sign. "It says so."

"What else would the ground be for?"

It was a good question. Derek told her he wasn't sure.

The girl started to laugh, then seemed to reconsider. She looked startled. "A sacred spot, maybe?"

"I don't think so. I guess we can sit here for a minute." They settled down and she dropped the four nickels onto the grass, carefully arranging them in a straight line.

"This is your grandmother," she said, drawing a circle with her finger around all the nickels. Then she took two away. "This is your mother." Again she made a circle with her finger around the remaining two nickels. Then she took another away. "This is you. You are only one-fourth Haida." She pressed the nickel into Derek's palm and closed his fingers around it. "It's not much. You have to listen closely to me, Ilyea, or you won't understand."

"What'd you call me—Ilyea?" Derek had opened his hand and was staring at the nickel, trying to make some sense out of what she was saying. The trouble was, in some ways it seemed natural for her to call him by another name since he'd always felt he was two people. Did this girl, who was also a whale, know the other boy inside him?

"You've got to listen carefully. I can tell you this only once." She told him about the legend: how Kitkune had saved the black whale and how, in turn, the black whale had saved her son, Ilyea. She told him how Ilyea learned to speak the black whale's language and how he became a great fishermen, the pride of his village.

Derek liked the story and he told her so.

"But this is not just a story." She pressed his hands around the nickel again. "You don't know anything about your own past, do you?"

"I've never heard that story before, if that's what you mean."

"This is going to be harder than I thought," she said, looking up to the sky. "I must send Kitkune to speak to your grandmother." Then she smiled at

Derek. "Please take this seriously," she said. "I'm trying to save my life."

"Can't you tell me what this is all about? I don't understand anything. Are you in danger? And why are you calling me Ilyea?"

The girl closed her hand firmly around Derek's and sighed. "I'm sorry," she said. "I'll try again. The Haida spirit lives five lives. When a Haida man or woman dies, that person's spirit is reborn in another's body. After the fifth time, the spirit becomes like the earth, knowing nothing. You are the fifth reincarnation of Ilyea, the great fisherman and friend of the black whale. . . ."

"But I can't be him," Derek interrupted her. "I don't even like to fish."

"That is why you often feel like two boys. Ilyea had no choice but to choose you, just as I have no choice."

This girl did know about both sides of him, Derek realized. Maybe she could help him solve his own mystery. Derek looked into her sad eyes and tried to concentrate on what she was saying.

"Think of yourself," she said quietly. "You know how it feels when the spirit and the body are not in harmony. But for me, it is much more urgent."

Derek looked closely at her face. Though she seemed full of life, her skin was pale, almost translucent;

he could even see the veins that throbbed at her temples.

"Unless you listen to Ilyea's spirit and help me find my way back to the sea . . ." She searched the ground with her eyes as if looking for something she'd lost. Finally, she pulled up a clump of grass with dirt clinging to its roots. "The plant needs the earth, just like the whale needs the ocean."

Derek took the handful of grass from her and patted it carefully back into the ground, hoping no one had seen her pull it up. "So you're saying that I . . ." Derek stopped. What could he offer a whale who could change herself into a young girl? She watched him as he tried to puzzle it out.

"Ahh," she said. "You're wondering why I don't do it myself, aren't you? Why I don't just wish myself there?" She shook her head sadly at him. "There are many things you don't understand yet. You are not looking at a human being. You are not looking at a being at all. You see a spirit in a form that you can understand. Don't I look familiar to you?"

Derek nodded. "Like my mom," he said, "when she was little."

"I thought that might please you. I am like your mother, too, in that I miss my son." She smiled sadly. "It is lonely here. Imagine, Ilyea, a world without voices or faces, a world where you cannot touch the people you love. Sometimes I feel like the old ones who have lost their senses."

Derek couldn't think. He tried to imagine what she said, but it seemed so horrible. He remembered watching the whales from the shore, the way the young ones stayed between their parents, the way the pods rested, their bodies close together.

"When the spirit strays from the body, the body weakens," she continued. "A spirit walks wherever it likes. But I cannot bring my body with me. As a spirit I could return to the ocean, but then, my body would die. I could never touch my children or love my mate in the same way again."

"You have children?" Derek asked. "Aren't you a little young?"

"Not for a whale," she said. "I'm eight in your years. But you are twelve, aren't you? Don't you have children yet?"

"No." Another time, Derek would have laughed at the idea, but he could see it was a logical question coming from her.

"What I don't understand is how I can help you. I'm just a kid."

"Yes. A kid. I don't know much about the world above the sea, but I do know that only children seem to recognize my spirit. Therefore, you must speak for me."

"You're the dolphin girl, aren't you?" Derek asked, remembering what Jerry had said about her only being visible to children.

"I protect my brother, the dolphin, sometimes. Yes."

"But I thought . . . don't black whales eat dolphins?"

"Yes, on occasion. What does that have to do with it?"

Suddenly, Derek didn't know. It seemed that everything he knew was being turned upside down. "You don't look like a witch," he said, instead of answering her question.

"When the children treat the dolphin unkindly, I appear to them in the form of a Haida maid, not a witch. The great cape and rain hat frighten them. But I don't want to frighten you." In the grass, she saw the whale carving where Derek had laid it when he sat down. She smiled, picking it up, and ran her fingers along the outline of its form.

"Can I ask you a question about me?" Derek asked.

She nodded.

"The first time I slept in our apartment, I woke up in the middle of the night. It was weird, like I was watching myself, but the me that was watching was laughing. He said, 'How can you sleep without the earth beneath you?' What could that mean?"

The girl thought for a moment. "Where was this apartment?"

"In Port Espadon."

"No, I mean where on the Earth? On a hill, by the shore?" Derek tried to describe it. The hardest part was explaining to her about the second floor.

"So you had earth, air, Ilyea?" She giggled. "That would be like water, air, me. I could not be comfortable there." Then suddenly, she got very quiet.

"What's the matter?" She shook her head, but Derek wouldn't let it go. "Please tell me."

"Once," she said finally, "when they were moving me off the airplane, my tank tipped. My head was underwater. I couldn't surface to breathe, and I felt what you humans call fear."

Derek tried to imagine what it was like to drown. "What do you want me to do?" he asked finally. The girl looked at him blankly for a minute, as if she'd forgotten everything she'd said before.

"Start with my trainer, Theresa," she advised. "Talk to her. You saw her this morning. You know she cares for me . . ." The whale girl broke off again, searching for words. "Oh, it's so hard to explain. Theresa thinks of me as a pet. You must make her think of me as a friend. I can't tell you how to do it. For that, you've got to listen to this." The girl handed him the whale carving. "There's powerful magic in it," she said. "Be careful how you use it."

"Hey, you kids! Can't you read?" An old man with a sunburned nose and a fishing cap pulled down to his bushy eyebrows drove up in a golf cart.

"Can you see me?" the girl asked him.

"Of course I can see you. I'm old, but I'm not blind."

"Isn't it extraordinary," she said to Derek. "Old people can see me, too. You are a very unique man. Tell me, can you speak to animals?"

"Me? No." He looked at the ground, then slowly wiped his hands on the front of his shirt. "I speak to plants, though."

"How?" Derek could see by the golf bag filled with rakes and hoes in the back of the cart that this man must be the gardener.

"With this." The gardener went to the back of his cart and pulled out a gleaming flute. "I play for them, see?" He blew a few clear notes on the pipe. "And they grow."

"It's you I've heard. Your music has been a great gift to me!" She reached forward to stroke the flute. "Tell us now about this sacred spot."

"Nothing sacred about it. You're just supposed to keep off."

"But why?"

"It's not grass for sitting. It's grass for decoration."

"Decoration?" Again, she laughed. Derek thought the whole embarrassing moment was almost worth it just to see her face light up.

"Sure. So it looks pretty and green and inviting."

"You made something people would want to sit on just so you could tell them it was wrong?" Derek wondered how long it had been since the old man was scolded.

"I guess that's one way to look at it," he said, as if he didn't understand it either.

"Well, I think that's silly," she answered back, staring him down. She turned away from him with a toss of her dark hair, and took Derek by the arm.

"You see what I mean? That's the way you humans are. Smart but not wise. You can make a beautiful thing, but you don't know how to use it." She started walking so fast that Derek almost had to run to keep up with her.

"But he saw you," Derek said. "That's good."

"Silly man." Then she seemed to reconsider. "He plays the most beautiful music, he must have a good heart." She stopped abruptly to admire a flowering lilac bush, immersing her face in the purple blossoms.

"What a lovely smell," she murmured, pulling her

head out again. "But I've got to get back." She resumed walking at the same quick pace. "Theresa will call the doctor again to inject me with appetite stimulants or some other ridiculous thing you humans have invented."

"You seem to know everything about me," Derek said, taking two steps to her every one. "I don't even know your name."

"You could not pronounce my name, so call me S'gana. That was the name given to us by the Haida people."

"S'gana," Derek repeated, trying to make it sound the way she had.

They reached the entrance to the stadium. A new sign was attached to the chain that blocked it: WHALE SHOW POSTPONED UNTIL 1:00 P.M. Theresa and another woman sat on the fiberglass platform, their legs dangling in the water. Derek crouched down to avoid being seen but S'gana rushed ahead, her straight hair flying behind her. Glancing at the two women, Derek could see that S'gana did not exist to them.

"I can't understand it," Theresa was saying. "Katy was fine this morning."

"You've been giving her the vitamins I prescribed?"

S'gana looked back at Derek and stuck out her tongue at the veterinarian's words.

"There was a kid this morning. Odd . . ." Theresa broke off and Derek strained to hear the rest of what she'd say.

"What was odd about it?" the doctor asked.

"Katy swam over to him as if she knew him; she seemed so happy to see him. When he ran off, she became like this again." Derek looked at the whale, who floated listlessly in the tank.

"I doubt that had anything to do with it, do you?"

"I don't know. But the fact that she's getting weaker and weaker is driving me crazy. I just wish we could figure out what it is."

"I'll do the best I can, Theresa, but we know so little about treating orcas. I'm limited in what I can do for her. I've got an appointment with Matt over at the pinniped exhibit now, but I'll check back later." Derek was relieved that she left without giving the whale any shots.

"What's the matter with you?" Theresa asked the whale, flipping water onto her huge back. She sniffed and wiped her nose with the back of her hand.

"I hate it when Theresa gets sad," S'gana said to Derek as she climbed up to the edge of the tank. "Now listen carefully. You've got to convince her that I need to go home."

"Home?" Derek realized he didn't even know where

home was for S'gana. The ocean was a big place. "Where's home?" he asked, but she ignored his question.

"Now that we know old humans can see me, your grandpa Joe's not a lost cause. Work on him, too. As for Tani . . ." S'gana stood, balancing on the side of the tank. "Ask her please, for S'gana, to leave the door open. Good luck, Ilyea." Then she dove into the water. Theresa must have heard the splash because she looked up.

"What was that?" she asked out loud. But then the whale came alive again. She swam over to Theresa and laid her big head in the trainer's lap. Then she swam to the center of the pool and executed a graceful arc above the water.

"All right!" Theresa shouted. Derek thought this was a good time to get out before S'gana blew the whistle on him again. He started to make his way out of the stadium, but she had other plans. The whale swam until she was just across from him and began making loud whistling and clicking noises.

"Not now," he whispered. "I need some time to think." But she only vocalized louder.

"Hey, you," Theresa said. "You're that kid! Don't leave." She took a step toward the water before she realized she'd have to go around the back. "Please, I

want to talk to you. You won't be in any trouble."
Theresa strode through the stage entrance.

Derek thought about running for it, but remembered the trainer's strong legs. He wouldn't get far. He straightened, stretching his legs, then slowly sat down on a stadium bench to wait for Theresa.

Six

A Sign

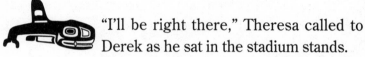 "I'll be right there," Theresa called to Derek as he sat in the stadium stands.

"This isn't going to be easy," Derek told S'gana, who had floated to the edge of the tank. She exhaled slowly, as if sighing in agreement.

When Theresa came over to him she seemed even taller than she had on stage. She wore jeans and a faded T-shirt with WHALE TRAINER on the front.

Holding out her hand to Derek, she said, "I'm Theresa, Katy's trainer. How do you do?" She gripped hard.

"Hi. I'm Derek Simpson."

"So, Derek . . ." Theresa sat down next to him and pulled one knee up close to her chest. "Tell me how you and Katy got to be such good friends."

Derek hesitated. If he began by telling her how he and S'gana met, Theresa would think he was crazy from the start.

"You're not feeding her anything, are you?" she asked, pointing to the whale carving that stuck out of Derek's pocket. He laughed.

"You don't think I go around with dead fish in my pocket, do you?"

She must have felt foolish for asking, because she blushed. "I guess not," she said.

"It's a carving of a whale that my grandmother gave to me." He pulled it out of his pocket and handed it to her.

Theresa took the carving and turned it over carefully. "This is Indian artwork, isn't it?"

"Yeah, my grandma's a Haida Indian." All of a sudden Derek saw the chance to make Theresa understand a little better. "It's a carving of a black whale, the same as Katy," he said. "To the Haida, black whales are sacred. They never interfere with them."

"That's interesting," Theresa said, handing the carving back to him. "I have a friend here who knows a lot about Indian art. I bet she could tell you if it's worth anything."

"No, thanks." Derek put the whale back in his pocket. "So how come you decided to be a whale trainer?"

"It was an accident, really," Theresa said. "In California, I worked for Ocean Park in crowd control, making sure the stadium didn't get overfilled and helping elderly people find seating. Anyway, Jeanette, the trainer at the time, slipped and broke her ankle right before a big show. The head trainer came out and asked me if I'd fill in for her. He said I wouldn't do any tricks or anything, just read the lines for the woman's part." Theresa walked over to the edge of the pool, grabbed a big rubber ring that hung from the side, and tossed it to the center. Slowly, Katy swam over to retrieve it.

"That was it? You didn't even want to be a trainer?" Katy brought the ring back to Theresa and exhaled, covering her with a fine mist.

"Hey," Theresa splashed water back at her. "The truth is," she turned back to Derek, "that I wanted to be a trainer more than anything else. That's why I always volunteered for crowd control. So I could be near Katy."

"What about the other lady?" he asked. "Didn't she want her job back?"

"Katy didn't like Jeanette. After that day, she wouldn't work with anybody but me. Isn't that right, Katy?" Theresa tapped the water, and Katy put her head over the side of the tank and opened her huge mouth so Theresa could rub her tongue. Then she slid back down in the water, pushing her head against the tank wall as if trying to get a better look at Derek.

"But now there's something wrong with her." When Theresa turned around, she had stopped smiling. "And I think you can help me figure out what it is." Behind her back, S'gana raised her head out of the water and moved it up and down as if to say, "Yes! Yes!"

It was at that moment Derek realized S'gana had a lot to learn about humans. This was too soon. Theresa wasn't going to believe a word of his story.

"I can tell you why she's sick," he said slowly, "but you won't believe me."

"Try me," Theresa said. S'gana leaped from the water, splashing them both when she came down.

"Okay," Derek shouted to S'gana over Theresa's shoulder. "She's not going to believe it, though." But S'gana refused to stop, making one high dive after another.

"If you don't mind, I'd like to know what's going on here."

Derek shrugged his shoulders. There was nothing left to do. So he told her. While he talked, Theresa listened carefully. She seemed to be concentrating very hard. At least she wasn't laughing. When he finished, she was silent for a long time. Even S'gana quieted down, though she kept her long body close to the tank wall.

"Why wouldn't this spirit, S'gana, speak to me?" Theresa asked him.

"Because you don't believe in her."

"How could I believe in something I didn't know *existed*?" Theresa asked, tossing the ring back into the water. "This is crazy. We're talking about a whale."

"That's just it. To you, she's only a whale. You won't be able to see S'gana unless you think of her as a friend."

Theresa started walking back and forth along the edge of the tank. "Why should I believe you? What proof do you have?"

"For one thing, she goes crazy every time she sees me," he said.

Theresa just looked at him.

"And you've heard about the dolphin girl? Well, she's really S'gana. Kids can see her, but adults can't."

Theresa sat down and rested her chin in her hands. "Even if I did believe you—and I'm afraid you're right, I don't—how do you think *I* could get Katy back to the ocean? We can't just buy her a plane ticket. Anyway, we'd have to sneak her out because *they*"—Theresa pointed in the direction of the park offices—"aren't about to let her go after paying thousands of dollars for her."

S'gana dove and swam to the other end of the pool.

"But she can't stay here," Derek persisted. "If she stays here, she'll die."

"What do you mean, she'll die?" Theresa asked sharply.

"Well, you were telling the doctor about how she gets quiet . . ." Derek walked over to the tank wall, and S'gana swam to him and rubbed her head against the glass. ". . . that's when her spirit leaves her body. S'gana is getting weaker. You know that."

"I don't want to talk about this anymore. I'm her trainer, and I decide what's best for Katy. Right now, I think it would be best if you don't come back here for a while. . . ."

"But it's not me. S'gana doesn't want to stay here, and if she has to die to get back, that's what she'll do."

Theresa shook her head. "Katy is *not* going to die. She's going to be fine." She pulled a whistle from her pocket and blew one high-pitched note with it. Katy didn't respond.

"I'm telling the truth." Derek started to lean over the edge of the tank so he could rub S'gana's back, but Theresa was right there. She yanked him backward.

"You're not to touch this whale. I'm telling you now to stay away!" She squeezed his arm tightly, and Derek struggled to get loose.

"You can keep me away from her, but you can't keep her away from me," Derek shouted at Theresa.

"I said, get out of here!" Theresa walked quickly to a red phone at the side of the stage.

Derek cupped his hands over his mouth to make sure Theresa couldn't hear him. "First thing tomorrow morning by the dolphin pool," he whispered to S'gana, waiting just long enough for her to nod before he ran.

Riding home with Joe was slow torture. Derek thought he'd bust if he couldn't tell someone who believed him about what had happened. But Joe didn't say a thing. He didn't even ask Derek how his day had been. It wasn't until they got to Arcadia that Joe finally said, "See any disappearing girls today?"

"Yeah, I saw her again. Right after I drank a big glass of lemonade."

They stopped at a light. Joe hit the brake a little hard. "What did she say this time?"

"She wants me to help her escape."

"Escape?" Joe turned to look at him. "From where?"

"From the park. She's the whale. Only she comes to me as a girl . . ." Derek stopped then, feeling foolish.

He knew his grandfather didn't believe him. The car behind them honked to tell Joe the light had turned green.

"I've heard about kids having invisible friends, Derek, but aren't you a little old for that?"

"I wish you wouldn't treat me like such a kid, Joe," Derek said, moving as close to the passenger door as he could.

"How do you want me to treat you, then? You *are* a kid."

"I don't know. Believe me once in a while."

They were silent the rest of the way home.

As soon as Joe walked in the door, he pointed a finger at Tani, who was pasting coupons into her green stamp book. "I want to talk to you in private."

Tani looked at him over her reading glasses. "Why?"

"Now."

Derek watched Joe march upstairs, then turned to Tani, who looked at him as if she were expecting an answer.

Derek just shrugged his shoulders. "All I did was tell him the truth." Slowly, he followed her up the stairs, then went to his room.

Tani and Joe argued loudly. Derek didn't want to listen, but when he heard Joe say, "I'm telling you, Tani, he's not going there anymore!" he found himself moving closer to the stair.

"And I'm telling you if he wants to go, he goes," Tani said firmly.

"You're the one who's been filling him with all this nonsense about whales and spirits."

"It's not nonsense," Tani said. "Derek's got a right to know. He's part Haida, after all."

"Then you can explain to Wiba why her son has invisible girlfriends who are really whales."

"Why don't you just believe what he tells you?"

"I've gotten this far in my life relying on my eyes and my common sense, that's why," Joe snapped.

"You've always been afraid of things you didn't understand, Joe."

"I'm telling you he's not going."

"He's going if I have to drive him there myself," Tani yelled.

"Well, that's just fine with me because *you* can't drive." Then a door slammed. When Derek came out of his room, Tani was putting on her reading glasses and smoothing back her hair.

As she passed him in the hall, she said, "When your grandpa goes to his lodge meeting after dinner, we'll talk."

Only Joe spoke as they ate dinner, carrying on as

usual about the farm report and the dry weather.

"Corn wasn't even knee-high by the Fourth of July," he said, digging into his pickled beets. "If we don't get rain the crops won't make it. Raspberries are smaller than my pinky," he grumbled.

"You're going to be late, Joe," Tani said as she splashed water onto the dishes.

Joe eyes went from Tani to Derek and back again. "I'm not going."

"What do you mean you're not going?" Tani came back to the table, drying her hands on her apron. Derek jumped up to help clear.

"Don't feel like it," he said. Derek knew it was just a way to keep him and his grandma from talking, and it made him mad that it worked. Joe kept them busy all evening playing cribbage, Yahtzee, and gin rummy. And long after they had all gone to bed, Derek, who kept creeping down the hall to look, could see his grandpa's reading light beneath the door.

The next morning, Derek was jolted awake as the sun broke through the curtains. It was after nine. How could he have slept so late? He threw on his clothes and tried to slick down the hair that always stuck up in the morning. Tani was in the kitchen drinking coffee and working on a crossword puzzle. She laughed at him when he came in.

"Your shirt's on inside out." She yanked it over his head and had it straightened around in no time.

"Tani," Derek said, tucking the tails into his shorts, "I've got to go today. It's important."

"I know it is. Joe just left or I'd have gotten you up long ago. I'm going to take you."

"But you can't drive."

"What the old man doesn't know hasn't hurt him for all these years, so I guess it can't hurt him now." She took Derek's hand and led him out to the garage. Joe's car was gone from the driveway.

"How are you going to drive us?" Derek asked, glancing at his grandma's watch. It was 9:30. The first whale show was at eleven. Derek remembered Theresa saying something about a show for the directors. If they were really the ones who ran the park, then it was important to see S'gana before then.

Tani walked quickly to the garage door and put a key in the padlock.

"Not Joe's antique wheeler car?" Derek started to back away. "He'll kill us."

"He won't kill us because he won't know." Tani threw back the doors of the old garage to reveal a Model T Ford. "During the Depression, I'd take it to the picture show while he was at work."

Derek had seen some of Joe's old cars at his

workshop, but this one was definitely the nicest. There wasn't a spot of rust on the gleaming grille.

Tani pulled a kerchief out of one apron pocket and a set of car keys out of the other. She untied her apron and dropped it on the front seat before wrapping the kerchief around her head. Then she disappeared inside the car. Derek heard the slow rumble of the engine. Tani called, "Get in, Derek. I'm out of practice, so we need to make time while we can."

The ride itself wasn't so bad. Derek soon got used to swaying back and forth when Tani started and stopped the car, and holding onto the passenger door when she took the turns. As they drove along the country road to Ocean Park, Derek looked at the crops Joe was talking about the night before.

"Harker took out all his corn and planted soybeans," Tani said, motioning to the hundreds of small green plants that grew in neat little rows. "There's almost nothing sadder than farm country during a drought," she said. "I just hope we get some rain soon."

When they reached the entrance to the park, Derek said, "Please come in with me. I want you to meet her. There are so many things I haven't told you."

"No, not now." Tani took his hand and squeezed it. "I have my reasons for not getting involved. But if I can't help you"—Tani reached across him and opened the door of the sedan—"at least I can keep Joe from stopping you. Now go. Do what you have to do and watch carefully for signs."

"Signs?"

"Anything can be a sign, Derek. The weather, a conversation. Signs can guide you."

"Okay. Thanks, Tani, I'll see you later." It wasn't until he was halfway to the dolphin pool that he realized he didn't know when Tani was coming back for him. But it didn't matter. Nothing mattered except seeing S'gana right now.

When he got to the pool, Derek couldn't find her anywhere. Had she already left? There were a number of children gathered around, throwing fish into the water. The dolphins faced the children, raising themselves out of the water just long enough to swallow the fish. One of the dolphins swam over to Derek and started making high-pitched cries. Derek held out his hand to show her he had no fish. But she wouldn't quit. Using her nose, she flipped water at him, then dove and swam to the far edge of the pool. When Derek didn't follow, she swam back and repeated the performance. Finally, he walked over to the far side of the pool near the booth where the fish were sold. The whale girl was peeking around the corner.

"S'gana?" Derek started walking toward her, but she held up her hand.

"Wait a minute," she said, studying him carefully. A moment later, she came out in an outfit identical to his.

"Oh brother, people are going to think we're twins," Derek said.

S'gana ignored him and walked over to the dolphin pool to dip her hands in the water. Suddenly, all the dolphins were at her side.

"Why do humans close us in like this?" she asked, caressing their sleek heads as they pushed forward to be touched.

S'gana couldn't concentrate near the dolphins, so they followed the path to the whale stadium and sat down to rest near the same patch of grass where they had talked the day before. Derek looked around. The gardener was nowhere in sight.

"Why do humans wear clothes?" S'gana asked, digging at the waistband of her shorts. "They're so uncomfortable." She sighed. "I've been thinking about yesterday and why it went the way it did. The problem is, you're just a kid."

"Wait a minute," Derek said. "Yesterday, I was perfect because I was a kid. Now that's the problem?"

"Don't you see?" S'gana grabbed Derek's arms. "Theresa doesn't believe you because you're not someone she looks up to. You should be older, maybe even a grown-up . . ."

"Since when do I need to be grown up to talk to someone about setting you free?"

"I don't think you do. It's what humans think."

"I wanted to tell you about that yesterday, S'gana. You're not human, and you don't know them as well as I do. So how about leaving the humans to me, okay?" S'gana was watching her hands as they traveled across the surface of the grass, but Derek knew she was listening.

"It's more complicated than it seems," he went on. "I'm pretty sure Theresa thinks she is taking good care of you. She really does care about you, S'gana."

"How can you care about someone and not understand her?"

"I don't know." He sat back. He was going to need a plan. Part of what S'gana had said was right. He could only get her free if he had some power. But all they had to do was throw him out of the park and it would be all over.

"Today's the show for the directors, isn't it?" Derek asked S'gana.

She nodded.

"Okay then, I have a plan." He didn't have a plan, really. He had a start, an inkling, an idea. Derek told

S'gana what he had in mind.

"If they think I have control over you, they'll listen. We'll just have to convince them that you won't perform for anyone but me."

"I hope you're right, Ilyea," she said. "You'll have to be very brave." Then S'gana did a very strange thing. She tried to stick her finger into Derek's mouth.

"Hey!" He pushed her away. "What do you think you're doing?"

"I was going to rub your tongue," she said, looking hurt.

"What would you want to do a thing like that for?"

"Because when I'm a human I can. See?" S'gana stuck her finger into her own mouth and rubbed it back and forth across her tongue. "Humans like to rub whale tongues. It's how they show affection."

"Well, we don't do that to each other."

"What do you do?"

"I don't know. Kiss, I guess."

"Kiss," S'gana said, pronouncing it slowly, "is a nice word. When I kiss Theresa in the show, I press my tongue against her face. Is that how you kiss?"

"Not exactly."

"How, then?"

There was no way he was going to show her how to kiss. He'd rather face the directors. "We don't have time for that now," he said, backing away from her. "You've got to get ready for your show."

"All right. But I won't forget that you owe me a lesson. Good-bye." He watched her walk away and disappear into the crowd.

After she was gone, Derek sat back down on the ground. He looked around to see if anyone was nearby before sticking his finger into his mouth. First, he rubbed it up and down, then back and forth. It tickled a little, but it was hardly worth the effort.

"Hey, kid." Derek jerked his finger out of his mouth. The gardener was driving up in his golf cart.

"You okay? You look kind of funny."

"Yes, sir, I'm fine."

"Call me Peter. Peter Montgomery's the name." They shook hands, and Derek waited to be scolded for sitting on the grass. But instead, Peter said, "I been thinking a lot about what you said yesterday. You know what? It made sense. What's the use of a nice patch of grass if you can't sit on it?" Peter pulled off his cap and scratched his head.

"I don't know." Derek tried to get a look at Peter's watch. "I don't want to be late for the whale show."

"Starts in a few minutes, I think." Peter glanced at his watch. "Anyway, I wanted to let you know I'm taking down the sign." He reached behind Derek and pulled the stake from the ground. Then he tossed the sign in the back of the cart. "And if Mr. Beaman doesn't like it, well, then let him explain it to all the kids who want to sit there."

"That's great, Peter," Derek said. As he hurried over to the stadium, he felt sure this was what Tani was talking about. A sign that even adults could change, if only they understood.

The girl selling lemonade had just finished unloading a crate of lemons as Derek passed by. She was about to break up the crate and toss it in the garbage when Derek had another idea. He was going to need a platform of his own. Maybe the crate would do. She gave it to him willingly and, with crate in hand, he ran down the path to the stadium.

Seven

The World Is as Sharp as a Knife

Derek entered from the back of the stadium to avoid being seen. Even so, he felt conspicuous. Most of the seats were empty for this first weekday show, so it was easy to spot the directors. He'd never seen so many suits, jackets, skirts, and blazers in the park at one time. They looked uncomfortable in their clothes, tugging at their collars and readjusting their skirts. He left the crate behind the sound booth for the time being and found a seat close to the directors.

Mr. Beaman, the man Derek had seen at the dolphin pool, had just entered near the whale tank. He, too, was wearing a suit. He walked quickly up the aisle.

"How are you, Mr. Carpenter?" Mr. Beaman asked a pale, slight man in a gray suit. "Did you have a nice trip?"

"Adequate," Mr. Carpenter replied. "I don't eat anything, you know. That helps with the jet lag."

From the conversation, Derek learned that the directors came from all over: Canada, California, Florida—there was even a woman from Japan. He also learned that Mr. Beaman was director of the Wisconsin Ocean Park, and had invited the other directors to come watch S'gana perform. This new show was more important than Derek had thought. For the first time, Derek realized he would soon be the center of attention. He remembered the last time he had been on stage, when he sang in the school choir. Each practice, he would manage to work his way a little farther back in the tenor section until he found the perfect spot, right behind Johnny Bateman's head, where he could sing unseen, pretending the crowd didn't exist.

But now Derek could not afford to be self-conscious. S'gana's life was at stake.

"This is a whole new concept in whale performance," Mr. Beaman began, as soon as everyone had quieted down. "We're trying to break free from trick-oriented shows and do something more interactive."

"Please explain that," the Japanese woman requested.

"Well, for lack of a better word, let's call it a dance."

Some of the directors laughed.

"A dance with a whale?" Mr. Carpenter asked. Mr. Beaman looked nervously at the stage, then sat down without saying anything more. Derek could tell he was taking a chance with his new idea and wanted to impress these people, not make them laugh.

Derek tried to concentrate on what he had to do. If he simply interrupted the show, Mr. Beaman would look like a fool and would never want to help out. But if he were to show them that he alone could get S'gana's attention, there was no better time than here and now in front of all these witnesses.

Watching Mr. Beaman, Derek guessed that Mr. Carpenter must be the most important director. If Derek could impress Mr. Carpenter and make it all look like Mr. Beaman's idea, then Mr. Beaman would have to take him seriously. Derek thought for a moment. Then, as the first strains of music came over the loudspeaker, he slid quietly out of his seat and left the stadium. He was looking for something, he didn't know what. Some way to single out Mr. Carpenter. As he rounded the corner to the dolphin-petting pool, Derek saw Peter again, tending one of his gardens. He rushed over to him.

"Peter, I need a favor."

"Whoa! Slow down, kid. Aren't you missing the show?"

"Would you give me some flowers, Peter? I can't explain now, but I . . ."

Peter chuckled. "You don't have to explain anything. I bet they're for your girlfriend, aren't they?" He pulled some pruning shears from his cart.

"Sort of," Derek said, because in a way they were for S'gana, even if she *wasn't* his girlfriend. "Whatever you've got is fine."

"You don't have to be shy with me, Derek. For her, I'd take roses. Feisty little thing. These will impress her." Peter led him to the back of the garden, where a brick wall had been covered with latticework. "I've been meaning to prune these anyway," he said, referring to a mass of climbing roses. He cut off several deep red blooms and handed them to Derek.

"I'll pay you back somehow. Thanks," Derek called over his shoulder.

"No need," Peter waved. Derek broke into a run. There was no time to lose.

When he got back to the stadium, Theresa and S'gana were about halfway through their dance. He had decided to let Theresa finish enough of her original program so the directors could see how hard she and S'gana had practiced. That meant waiting until his favorite part, when Theresa rose out of the water on one of S'gana's fins, just like a ballerina.

As he picked up his crate, Derek realized he would need some help if the directors were to believe that his part of the show had been planned.

The door to the sound booth was partially open. A man wearing headphones was adjusting the volume for a new piece of music, the last one for the segment. Derek knocked on the door, and the man pushed his headphones down so they rested on his neck.

"What do you want, kid?" he asked, irritated.

"There are some changes . . ." Derek began.

"What?" He put one headphone to his ear and flicked another switch.

"There are some changes. Just try to follow me."

"Changes? Who said changes?" Derek heard the scattered applause of the small audience and watched S'gana rise from the water holding Theresa.

"Mr. Beaman knows about this, and he wants your help. Do the best you can." With that, he grabbed his crate and flowers and scooted around to the front of the booth. He waited, squatting below the window so the soundman couldn't see him.

Theresa was on stage, smiling and bowing. S'gana was halfway out of the water, moving her upper body back and forth as if she, too, were bowing. Derek slowed his breathing to get ready before standing up.

Theresa spoke into her microphone, "I give you

Katy, the seventh wonder of the world."

Derek hurried down the center steps with the flowers hidden under his crate, and rapped on the tank wall. S'gana, who had been racing back and forth beneath the surface, stopped mid-tank and floated to the surface.

"Katy, the seventh wonder of the world," Theresa repeated louder. Derek watched Theresa scan the audience, until their eyes met. He glanced over his shoulder at the directors, who were murmuring among themselves. Mr. Beaman started tapping his fingers on the metal armrest. Taking a deep breath, Derek set his crate down and stood on it so that most of his body was above the clear divider. When he raised both his arms, S'gana suddenly came alive again, diving deep and executing a high leap from the water, clearly higher than even Theresa had ever seen.

For a moment, she stared at the whale. Then her eyes moved to Derek. She was shocked. He had ruined her show, and there was nothing she could do about it. Even if she had him taken away, S'gana would most likely just go back into her trance.

Derek put both his arms down, then lifted his left arm. S'gana swam to the left side of the pool and did a neat leap and breach to the left, splashing the people seated nearby. It was a sure-fire crowd pleaser. The audience screamed, trying to duck behind one another for cover. Derek repeated the command with his right hand. A burst of organ music accompanied each leap. Except to those who knew better, the whole performance looked as though it had been planned.

When Derek started to run out of ideas, S'gana filled in the gaps by swimming near him and lifting her head over the side of the tank to smile at the children. They waved to her and giggled, but whether it was out of delight or fear, Derek couldn't tell. He reached over and stroked S'gana's head tentatively, still a little afraid of her himself. It was the first time he had ever touched a whale, and he was surprised at how smooth her skin felt, like the cool, black inner tubes he used to float the river back home.

"What now?" he wondered and, as if she had heard him, S'gana's voice echoed in his ears: *Dance.*

Derek thought of all the dances that he knew. He had learned some disco in gym class once. But that didn't seem appropriate. He and his mother would sometimes slow dance at weddings. That hardly seemed right either. Finally, he remembered a dance that might work. He turned around to face the audience.

"S'gana wants to learn to hula," he shouted, his voice echoing through the near-empty stadium.

"Everybody stand up. Maybe we can help her." He deliberately kept his eyes off the directors. The thought of Mr. Beaman peering down at him made him nervous.

"How about some music?" he called out, and was answered with a nice, slow, piped-in version of Hawaiian sound. Derek turned around again on his little crate, and holding both hands over to the left side of his body, began swaying his hips in time to the music.

He felt pretty foolish about the whole thing. S'gana did her best to imitate him. She held one pectoral down and stuck the other one straight out. Then she swayed back and forth in that direction. It was a human dance, after all. Behind him, Derek heard the audience laughing. He was sure it must be at his expense; but when he turned around, he saw that the children were nudging each other with their hips and flapping their arms to the side, imitating the whale. Even the directors seemed to be loosening up. Everyone was having a good time. Everyone except Theresa, of course, who had all but disappeared from view. Every now and then Derek caught a glimpse of her in the shadow of the stage door.

When the music stopped, Derek turned around again. He had run out of dances.

"Any requests?" he asked.

"How about the hokeypokey?" someone called from the back. Derek squinted to see who had called it out. Peter Montgomery, the gardener, was standing at the back entrance. "That's always been a big favorite of mine!" he shouted. Derek waved to him. He had never felt happier to see anyone in his whole life. Several members of the audience voiced their approval by clapping and whistling.

"Okay," Derek agreed. "But we're going to have to do the whale hokeypokey." He put his hands under his armpits and shook his left elbow. "That's the left fin . . ." Then he shook his right. "Then the right fin, head, and tail. Got it?"

"Yes," several people shouted. Derek turned back to S'gana.

"Okay, music!" he called. "You put the left fin in, you put the left fin out . . ." S'gana was doing just fine, following right along with the movements. "You put the left fin in and you shake it all about. You do the hokey-pokey and you turn yourself around. That's what it's all about. Hey!" When Derek turned around he was surprised to see everyone joining in, even Mr. Carpenter.

The audience laughed and turned and shook from the right fin and then the head. When they got to the tail, S'gana delighted everyone by diving almost all the way underwater and shaking her tail for all it was worth. Then she made a high leap and splashed down for the final "Hey!" covering Derek with water.

"Thanks, S'gana," Derek whispered before calling out to the audience. "There's just one more thing we've got to do today. S'gana wants to give something to Mr. Carpenter, one of Ocean Park's very special guests." Derek got off his crate and reached underneath it for the bouquet. He selected the prettiest flower with the straightest stem and said, "Why don't you take it to him, S'gana?"

She rose slowly out of the water and took the stem carefully between her teeth. Swimming in the direction that Derek indicated, she stuck her head out over the partition and waited patiently.

Mr. Carpenter stepped up to her quickly. He was chuckling to himself and wiping at his eyes under his glasses. He took the rose and held it up for the audience to see before breaking the stem and inserting it into his lapel. There was a loud round of applause.

"Well, that about wraps things up," Derek said. He was about to step down from his crate and take what was coming to him, but S'gana dove beneath the surface. "I guess S'gana's not finished yet," he told the audience. Then, once more, he heard her voice in his ear.

Kiss. At the same moment, the whale rose out of the water and pressed her great tongue to the side of his face.

When the cheering subsided, Derek gathered up his crate and the rest of the flowers and walked up the steps to Mr. Beaman. The man looked positively furious, but he wasn't saying a word. How could he? The voices around him were overwhelming.

"Absolutely loved it," Mr. Carpenter was saying. "What an amazing discovery. A child trainer. I'll recommend it for California."

"How'd I do, Mr. Beaman?"

"You certainly did, didn't you," was all Mr. Beaman could say.

The Japanese woman patted Derek on the back. "You were very good."

" . . . can't get over it . . . had us all fooled . . . the other one was all right as well, but the kid here—"

"Beaman, you're brilliant. They're going to *love* this in California."

Derek just smiled up at Mr. Beaman and waited.

"What am I thinking?" Mr. Carpenter exclaimed, looking at his watch. "We're a half-hour late for the airport. Quick, everyone," he began herding the other directors into the aisles, "to the limos." As they started to file out, Mr. Carpenter turned back to Mr. Beaman.

"Why don't the two of you ride out with us, Bob? I want to spend some more time with this amazing child." He smiled down at Derek.

"I'd love to, but we still have some contractual arrangements to work out."

"I understand," Mr. Carpenter winked at Mr. Beaman. "Get him to sign before someone else snatches him up. But Bob . . ."

"Yes, sir?"

"Work on the props, will you? He needs a little costume or something. And a podium." Mr. Carpenter waved his hand at Derek's crate. "Tacky."

Mr. Beaman put his arm around Derek. "Yes, sir. I'll see to that, sir." To Mr. Carpenter, they must have looked like a friendly pair. Only Derek could feel how tight Mr. Beaman's grip was on his shoulder. When the directors were out of sight, Mr. Beaman turned Derek around and marched him to the front of the stadium. He unlocked a door at the side of the stage and, pushing Derek in front of him, walked up to another door with *THERESA* painted on it. He knocked.

"Come in." Theresa had her back to them, lifting a big barbell over her head. As soon as she saw Derek, however, she dropped it to the floor and shouted, "Just what the hell did you think you were doing?"

"Let's back up a minute," Mr. Beaman said, pushing

Derek into a straight-backed chair. "Just who the hell *are* you?"

"His name is Derek," she said.

"You know him?" Mr. Beaman sighed, and leaned back against the wall.

"Not really."

"Why did you do this, son?" Mr. Beaman asked him softly. "And when and how did you teach that whale all those tricks?"

"I didn't teach her the tricks. We never practiced that before. She just followed my lead."

Mr. Beaman looked over at Theresa. "You're not in on this, are you?"

"Of course not. You might as well tell him your story, Derek. I assume that's what you're here for." She poured herself a glass of water and drank it down in one long swallow.

"The whale has to go back to the ocean," Derek said. "Otherwise, she'll die."

"What do you mean? She's perfectly healthy." Mr. Beaman opened a side door and walked out to the stage. Derek and Theresa followed him. S'gana was halfway up the slide-out platform. She looked as if she had been listening.

"That's not exactly true, Bob," said Theresa. "I was talking to Doc Barnes about it yesterday. Katy's losing

weight. Last week, she was running a temperature."
Theresa sat down next to S'gana, dangling her legs in
the water.

"How do *you* know about all this?" Mr. Beaman
asked Derek.

"Because she told me."

"You know the whale's health is confidential information, Theresa." Mr. Beaman almost lost his footing
on the slippery stage. He recovered himself and walked
slowly backward, grabbing onto the stage door.

"The whale told him, Bob, not me."

"I see. The whale told him." Mr. Beaman straightened his shoulders. Derek noticed that his shirt collar
bit into his neck. The idea of whales talking to humans
was clearly upsetting him. Derek felt sorry for this
man, just as he felt sorry for his grandpa. What a
boring world if all you ever thought about was what you
could see.

As if he understood what Derek was thinking,
Mr. Beaman took off his jacket and tossed it over the
tank's retaining wall. He loosened his collar and rolled
up his sleeves. Then he found an empty fish bucket,
turned it over, and sat down on it.

"I still don't know just who you are."

Derek sighed. "Part of me is Derek Simpson. That's
who you see. But another part of me is a boy named

Ilyea. He was a Haida fisherman who lived a long time ago. Ilyea was a friend of the black whale, a friend of S'gana, here." S'gana, who had slid back into the water by this time, slapped her tail on the surface.

"S'gana? That's an Indian name, isn't it?" Derek nodded, and Mr. Beaman looked relieved to have cleared up at least one matter.

"Letting the whale go is out of the question, son. You see, even if I wanted to, I couldn't do it. It's not my decision to make. However . . ." he took a deep breath and glanced over at Theresa. "I think we could arrange for you to see her more often."

"What?" Theresa stood up and began rubbing her legs briskly with a towel.

"Theresa, you saw how Carpenter ate him up. There's no way around it."

"You can do whatever you want, Bob. Just count me out." Mr. Beaman opened his mouth as if to answer, but nothing came out. Theresa walked as far as the back-stage door, but Derek knew she would stay to see what happened. She cared about S'gana too much.

"How would you like to work for Ocean Park, Derek?" Mr. Beaman asked him, keeping his eyes on Theresa's back.

"Thank you for the offer, sir," Derek said slowly. "But I'm not interested in working for you. I'm here to help S'gana get back home."

"He's the *cause* of all our problems, not the solution, Bob," Theresa said, coming back to center stage. "Every time Katy gets sick, I find him lurking around. I don't pretend to understand the kind of power he has over her. All I know is, if we got rid of him maybe things would return to normal."

"Why can't you see what S'gana's asking?" Derek shouted back at her. "All she wants is her life back! All she wants is to be free. If she dies, it'll be *you* who killed her!"

Mr. Beaman looked at each of them and shook his head. There was only one thing to do. "I'm afraid you leave me no choice, Derek. I'm going to have to ban you from the park."

"What? You can't do that."

"I can do whatever I like. This is private property, you know. And right now, you're trespassing."

The words were clear enough, but Derek couldn't bring himself to believe them. If he was being kicked out for good, would he ever see S'gana again?

His plan had failed. Derek glanced over at the tank. S'gana floated quietly at the other end, blowing her mist high into the air every few minutes.

"I'll keep Derek in my office until we can get someone to pick him up," Mr. Beaman told Theresa.

"I'll find a way to meet you again, S'gana." The words came out in a rush. "Don't worry," Derek said, but at the moment, he didn't really believe it himself. Theresa wouldn't look at him. Was that a good sign?

Mr. Beaman led Derek to the edge of the stage before Theresa spoke, and then it was only to say, "Don't forget your jacket, Bob." Quick as a flash, S'gana swam over to it and, pushing out of the water, grabbed it between her teeth. Then she dove below the surface and reappeared in front of Derek and Mr. Beaman with the wet, wrinkled mass in her mouth. Silently, Mr. Beaman reached down to take the jacket.

"When did you teach her that?" he asked Theresa. In spite of everything, Derek had to laugh. Theresa was laughing too, though she tried not to.

As they reached the entrance to the stadium, Derek glanced up to see S'gana sitting in the bleachers, her head in her hands.

"I'll be back," he called to her.

"I doubt that," Mr. Beaman answered, guiding Derek along with a hand on his shoulder.

"Please, Ilyea . . . will you try again?" Derek hated the pleading tone of her voice. "This time start with the weakest link. Start there . . . and use the whale."

Derek wanted her to explain, but Mr. Beaman pulled him out of hearing range.

After they had gone, Theresa sat again at the edge of the pool. "I've always done what I thought was right for you," she told the whale. "I made sure you had the best diet, the most comfortable conditions. I've stayed with you constantly. What more could you want?" she asked, shaking her head.

Suddenly, S'gana, who had been floating quietly on the surface, lunged toward her, frightening Theresa for the first time since she had become the whale's trainer. Opening her great mouth, she surrounded Theresa's legs and brought her top teeth down. Theresa gasped. It all happened too quickly for her to move. But S'gana stopped when her teeth reached Theresa's skin. Slowly she slid her teeth along Theresa's legs, all the way to her feet. She did this so gently it felt to Theresa like an itch being scratched. When it was over, S'gana swam again to the other side of the pool.

Trembling, Theresa pulled her legs from the water. There wasn't a mark on them.

It was Joe who picked Derek up from Mr. Beaman's office. They had to wait while Mr. Beaman got the park photographer to take Derek's picture.

"Don't think you can sneak in, young man," Mr. Beaman said to Derek. "I intend to have this picture posted at every ticket booth and entrance gate."

Mr. Beaman then handed Joe a check for the amount of a season pass.

"Thank you, Mr. Beaman," Joe said solemnly, and they shook hands. "And I'm sorry for whatever trouble Derek's caused."

"I wouldn't be too hard on the boy," Mr. Beaman said, shuffling through a stack of telephone messages on his desk. "He may be misguided, but he seems to really believe in what he's doing. We take good care of Katy here at Ocean Park, Derek." As if to prove this, he motioned to a wall of photographs full of smiling costumed whales and real whales planting kisses on people's cheeks.

"Would *you* be happy in a cage?" Derek asked him.

Mr. Beaman shook his head. "It's not like that at all here," he said, looking Derek in the eye for the first time since they had come to his office. Then he turned to Joe. "I have a son Derek's age in Little League. A fine organization. Maybe if you kept him busy, the boy would forget all about this."

"Thanks for the advice," Joe said, his hand on the door. "We'll make sure he doesn't bother you again."

Joe waited until they were on the county road before he said, "This has gone too far, Derek. You can never go back to the park again. Do you understand?"

"Yes, sir." Derek slouched down in his seat.

Things couldn't get much worse. He was beginning to understand what Tani meant about the world being sharp as a knife.

At home, there was a package on his bed from his mother, the one she had promised him. Derek pushed it aside at first, but then returned to it. He didn't want to think about this afternoon. Opening the box, he found a letter.

"I know I'm a bad mother. This package is so late. But I had the hardest time thinking of anything you would really want. I understand—part of me wanted to leave everything behind in the apartment and start our new life with a clean slate.

"But there are some things worth keeping and worth passing down from mother to son. Hundreds of years ago, you would have had this blanket to keep you warm on hunting trips. On the back is Raven, the trickster, but also the source of all life.

"It's been so hot there the last thing you need is a blanket, but something told me to send it, so I did. They used to say if you wrapped yourself inside this blanket, you could feel its magic. Do you believe in magic? I think I do."

There were a few more pages, but Derek stopped reading. He reached into the box and took out his mother's button blanket, still musty from the attic.

Laying it out on the bed, he saw the outline of Raven, his wings stretched and his head turned to one side. Shiny beads and buttons decorated his form. Underneath the blanket his mother had packed all sorts of familiar things. There was a trophy he had won years ago in a swimming contest, an old pack of playing cards, his gum-wrapper chain, and a set of marbles he and his mom used to shoot in the kitchen together. Derek fingered the cat's-eye before setting everything on his dresser. Just looking up at them made him feel more at home.

What would his mom say about all this? More than anything, he wanted to tell her, but Joe had asked him not to mention "the whale business" to her. He wondered what Joe was afraid of. That his mom would think Joe and Tani weren't taking good care of him? He lay down on the bed and, pulling the blanket over him, thought about S'gana's last words. What could she have meant by "start with the weakest link" and "use the whale"? He stared at the carving on his dresser, but nothing came to him. If he ever needed to believe in magic, now was the time.

Eight

Whale Magic

The next few weeks were the worst Derek had ever spent. Tani didn't speak to Joe; Joe didn't speak to Tani, except when he had to; and Derek only spoke to Joe when Joe spoke first.

Mr. Beaman was wrong. Derek couldn't forget about S'gana. He was worried sick about her. He watched the television news every night to see if she had done something awful or taken sick. He had never felt so helpless and alone in all his life.

When Derek told Tani what had happened, she just sighed and said, "Maybe they're right, Derek. Maybe we shouldn't try to interfere with the way things are." Tani was the one person Derek thought would never let him desert S'gana.

Derek started sitting outside on the steps that led

down to Joe and Tani's backyard. Long after everyone was asleep, he would sit watching the stars, wrapped in his mother's button blanket. Though the nights were warm, he often felt chilled. He started sending S'gana messages with his thoughts, messages of hope and encouragement. At first, he told her he just needed a little time to come up with another plan. But after a while, the thoughts refused to form in his mind. "Dear S'gana," he said aloud as if composing a letter. "I haven't forgotten you, but I don't know what to do next. I guess I'm asking for a miracle. Do whales believe in miracles?" Derek could ask S'gana to have hope for only so long. Finally he pushed the blanket off his shoulders. There wasn't any magic in his past, he decided.

It was a hot, dry night. It hadn't rained for weeks and no rain was expected. Everything was curling up, turning brown, and dying in the heat. It was a time when people like Joe and Tani thought mostly about their own problems. Maybe they didn't have room in their hearts for the problems of a lonely whale.

Derek watched the moon and the stars in the clear, dark sky and wondered if the night cared about S'gana. He saw a shooting star, but it didn't excite him. On nights like this at home, when he watched the sky from his window, the other Derek would almost always visit him, the one he now knew as Ilyea. Ilyea would laugh and ask him why he let the house come between him and the stars. Derek wondered where Ilyea was now, and why he'd felt his presence so little since he'd met S'gana.

He went back inside to get the whale carving from his dresser. Seated on the steps again, Derek turned the shiny figure over and over in his hand, repeating S'gana's words: "Start with the weakest link. Use the whale." What could she mean?

It wasn't until dawn that it came to him. The carving had given him the strength to do what had to be done. He'd always been shy, but he had stood in front of a crowd of strangers and danced the hokeypokey. Derek squeezed the carving and felt the cool stone against the warmth of his palms. This whale really did have strong magic. It had helped him see what was right and believe it was possible to get S'gana back to the ocean.

A chain is only as strong as its weakest link. Tani must be that weak link. But Tani was his strongest supporter. If she hadn't believed him from the beginning, he could never have come this far. Why had she changed her mind now?

Had Tani lost some of her power when she gave him the carving? Derek was sure that if Tani could only be brought back over to his side, they could free S'gana.

The next morning, Derek and Tani were clearing the breakfast dishes. Another somber meal was over. Joe had left to inspect the fairgrounds, without even saying good-bye. Derek didn't want to go, but it hurt him just the same that Joe hadn't asked.

Tani scraped the leftovers into a small can for her compost bin by the back garden. Derek washed and rinsed the dishes and set them in the drainer. When they were finished, Tani passed Derek the towel to dry off his hands. He took the whale carving from his pocket, set it in the middle of the towel, and returned it to her.

"I guess I won't be needing this anymore," he said, watching her closely. Tani didn't look at him. She unwrapped the whale carefully and polished it with the dish towel.

"I meant this as a gift." She handed it back.

"No," Derek said firmly, pressing the whale into her hands. "You said that it might help me to understand. Now it only hurts me to look at it. I don't want to carry it with me anymore."

"All right." She put the whale carving in her apron pocket and, turning away from him, busied herself putting things back into the refrigerator.

Derek sat down at the kitchen table, tracing patterns with his finger, watching Tani hang up her apron and carefully take the whale out again.

"There's something I don't understand about all this," Derek said.

"What's that?" Tani looked at him warily.

"Well . . ." he paused, imagining the magic from the little carving soaking into her skin. "It's something S'gana said to me about you once."

"About me?" Tani poured herself a cup of coffee from the pot on the stove and sat down at the kitchen table with Derek. One by one, she lifted unfolded napkins from a laundry basket at her side and smoothed them out on the table.

"Remember the story that S'gana told me about Kitkune and Ilyea?"

"Yes."

"Well," said Derek, "there was a part I didn't tell you. S'gana was angry that you hadn't told me about my past."

"Maybe for the Black Whale People things have not changed. But for the Haida they have. How could we pass on the stories of our ancestors when our elders died before they could tell them, and the children died before they could hear them?"

Tani seemed angry with Derek, but it didn't

really bother him. He had to find out why she wasn't helping him.

"I thought," he said slowly, "that maybe you'd just know them. You'd be born knowing them."

Tani set the whale down between them on the table. "In my grandmother's time," she said, "the government outlawed our feasts, our celebrations, our customs. I was born a Haida, but without the knowledge of what that meant.

"My mother tried to teach me and my brother Kwung the things her grandmother had taught her. Don't get me wrong, Derek. We were happy for a long while. We played outside every day, my brother and I. We made friends with the trees, the animals. We gathered reeds for making baskets and helped dry the fish. We were happy until we had to go to missionary school.

"They separated the boys from the girls there, and we couldn't see each other all day. There was a yard for playing. Imagine. My brother, Kwung, who roamed for miles before breakfast, was supposed to keep inside a small, dusty play yard. He kept jumping the wall and finding his way out to the creek that ran behind the school. When the headmaster found him, my brother got whipped.

"Kwung and I would still find time to sneak off so

we could see each other. The other boys teased him about that, too, and he got in fights."

"Was that when Kwung first had problems?"

Tani nodded. "My mother couldn't control him. He grew into somebody I didn't know. He even went to jail for a while. Then, one night, he got into a fight in a bar and someone shot and killed him. I never understood how a person could change like that. I blamed it on the school for not allowing him to be himself. Kwung never blamed anyone. He kept telling me it was no one's fault, that he'd just been born at the wrong time.

"My mother couldn't get over it. We were all she had. I married your grandfather and moved away. I never saw my mother again. We killed her, Kwung and I." Tani kept her head down, sweeping crumbs from the table into her palm.

"But you couldn't help it," Derek insisted. "If anything, it was the school's fault. They killed your brother, not you."

"Passing the blame is too easy, Derek. As I said, Kwung felt he was born at the wrong time. He told me the spirit inside him made him yearn to live in the days when the Haida lived off the land and the sea . . ."

"Yes," Derek said. "I know how he felt."

Tani smiled. "You remind me of him, sometimes."

Tani finished her coffee and went to the sink to

rinse her cup. There were birds drinking from the small bath that hung from a tree just outside the window. Tani stood watching them for a long time.

"I know now that there were many things I could have done. But my punishment is that I did not do them."

"I don't understand," Derek said.

"I've spent my adult life trying to forget the past. That is why I can't see the black whale girl or feel the magic anymore." They were silent for a while. Finally, Tani picked up the whale carving and rubbed it against her cheek.

Derek was the first to speak. "There was one other thing S'gana wanted me to tell you. She said, 'Tell Tani, please, for S'gana, to leave the door open.' What does that mean, Tani?"

She smiled. "My mother used to say if we wanted the spirits to visit us, we had to leave the door open."

"S'gana wants Kitkune to visit you."

"Why would Kitkune want to visit me?" Tani asked. The idea must have pleased her a little because she ducked her head and pulled on her braid the way she did when Joe surprised her with a gift.

"I don't know," Derek said.

"It will never happen. But I'm grateful to you for helping me remember my good mother, Derek." She kissed him. Then she walked out of the room.

That evening, when Tani knew Joe was asleep, she tiptoed over to the dresser to retrieve her whale carving. She took it out of the drawer, where it lay wrapped in its soft cloth, and held it to her cheek. Then she hid it under her pillow, and before returning to bed, opened the bedroom door a crack.

Many visitors took advantage of Tani's open door that night—a tall, dark woman in a cone-shaped hat told her stories about the old ways. And Tani's own mother came to her in a long muslin skirt, an apron wrapped tightly around her small frame; she sat on the edge of Tani's bed stroking her daughter's hair.

When Tani awoke the next morning, she knew somehow she had been forgiven. It was Sunday, and she couldn't remember feeling so lighthearted since she'd been a young girl.

She slipped out of bed and dressed quickly, spraying a little rose water on her skin and tying a ribbon in her braid for church. The last thing she did before she left the room was to set the little whale on the dresser, where Joe would be sure to see it.

Tani knocked on Derek's door. Like Joe, he slept as late as he could on Sunday mornings. But he woke quickly when she entered the room and sat at the side of his bed.

"Thank you," was the first thing she said, hugging him tightly. "I know you gave me back the whale so that I would help S'gana, but she has helped me as well. "Did you know," she asked, smiling shyly down at him, "that Kitkune is part of me?"

Joe was straightening his tie in the mirror when he saw the whale carving. A moment earlier he had been whistling "Let Me Call You Sweetheart," but caught himself, remembering they no longer had fun around this house. That made him angry and the little whale made him even angrier.

He picked it up from the dresser and turned it over in his hand. He could tell from the flowing circles and U-shaped carvings it was Haida art, but he had never seen it before.

"Now why would the old woman keep this hidden away for so many years?" he asked himself. It put him in a mind to have a talk with her. Had she shown it to Derek? he wondered. All that boy could think about was whales, whales, whales ever since his first trip to Ocean Park. Joe looked at himself in the mirror. I'm an old man, he thought. Maybe Tani was right. Maybe the years hadn't made him any wiser.

"Joe, we're going to be late for church," Tani called from the foot of the stairs. He could hear her tell

Derek, "If a man could get dressed and go about his affairs for the day in a horizontal position, that's just what your grandfather would do." Her little joke gave Joe hope. Maybe Tani would snap out of it and start speaking to him again, even teasing him again. Joe put the carving into his jacket pocket, took his hat from behind the door, and hurried down the stairs.

Lately, most of Reverend Elsley's sermons had addressed the matter of the drought. Today, he focused on faith in the face of hardship.

Opening with Mark 11:23, he read in his deep, vibrant voice: "For verily I say unto you, That whosoever shall say unto this mountain, Be thou removed, and be thou cast into the sea; and shall not doubt in his heart, but shall believe that those things which he saith shall come to pass; he shall have whatsoever he saith."

Joe was reminded of a dream he had had the night before. He'd been having a hard time sleeping lately, and he knew he'd be fooling himself if he blamed it on the heat alone. Derek was in that dream, he realized now, and he was being chased off Ocean Park grounds by Mr. Beaman and several security guards.

The kneeler creaked, and Joe looked over to see Derek raising and lowering it with his foot. He touched the boy's shoulder. His grandson looked up at him and smiled. It was the first smile in at least a week.

Joe glanced around him. Old Mrs. Briard was nodding silently to the Reverend's words. Clem was smoothing down what was left of his hair. And little Weston Behling, his head bent over his coloring book, was making a purple sky. Joe smiled and leaned back against the pew. Without thinking, he slipped his hand into his jacket pocket and felt the whale carving.

"A faithful witness does not lie," the Reverend intoned, looking straight at Joe.

For a moment, Joe saw everything from Derek's point of view. Derek believed in the whale girl; he knew her. Maybe if Joe had faith in his grandson, then what he didn't understand now would be made clear to him. But he had to have faith.

"Thank you," said Joe, shaking Reverend Elsley's hand heartily after the sermon, "I think I understand now."

"I was wondering if I'd ever get through to you," the Reverend said, winking. Joe walked away, wondering what the Reverend meant. No matter, he thought, heading quickly back to the car. He knew what to do now.

"For the life of me, I can't understand your mood swings lately," Tani said as Joe opened the car door for her and kissed her hand. Even if she had known that the little whale carving was in Joe's pocket, she would not have believed its magic could work so fast.

"You don't have to understand, Tani. Just feel." He grabbed her around the waist and pulled her close to him, whispering in her ear.

"Joe!" Tani pulled away from him, though she was still smiling. "We just got out of church."

"Let's go dancing then," he suggested.

"At noon on a Sunday?"

"How about the back porch?" He rushed to the other side of the car and opened Tani's door with a flourish.

Later that afternoon in a family conference, Joe, Tani, and Derek decided that Theresa should have the whale carving for a while. Derek told them that she had once offered to have a friend find out how much it was worth. They decided that Joe would take it to her and ask her to have it appraised. Maybe if Theresa kept it around her house, she would come around to their way of thinking.

Ever since Derek had taken over her whale show, Theresa noticed that Katy was eating less than usual. Even worse, Katy was treating Theresa as if she hardly knew her. She never swam up to put her head on Theresa's lap and get her tongue rubbed. And she had stopped vocalizing. All Theresa heard during their practices now was her slow, measured breathing.

Theresa could see that something was really wrong with Katy, but she refused to believe what Derek had told her. "That kid has just worn you out," she told the whale. "I wish we'd never met him." She grabbed a few fish out of the training bucket, then slipped out of her sweat suit and into the water. "You don't really remember your life in the ocean, do you? That was years ago."

She dove down and kicked to the middle of the tank. The whale brushed against her. Good. For once, she wouldn't have to coax Katy to begin. When she reached her spot for the opening number, Theresa began to surface, but Katy swam above her. Theresa was pleased. Katy was playing with her again. She pushed on the whale's underside, trying to swim around her, but Katy swam to the side, too.

It dawned on Theresa that Katy might be intentionally trying to keep her from swimming to the surface, but she dismissed the thought. Katy would never hurt her. Trying to remain calm, Theresa grabbed one of Katy's pectoral fins to pull herself along the whale's body to the surface. Katy rolled so that her fin dropped deeper into the water. Theresa waved the fish in front of Katy's mouth, but Katy ignored them. Dropping the fish, Theresa swam and kicked as hard as she could to get away from the whale, but Katy's shadow stayed over her.

She begged Katy to let her surface. "I need air!" she screamed in a stream of bubbles, and pounded Katy's side with her fists. Soon after that, she lost consciousness.

When she came to, Theresa found herself halfway up the slide-out platform. No one else was around. It took her a long time to remember what had happened. But even when she did, she refused to believe Katy had tried to kill her. After all, Katy must have pushed her onto the platform to save her life.

Then why did Katy do it? Maybe Katy *was* playing. But if so, how did she know when to stop? Theresa stood up slowly. Katy swam near her, turning her body to the side so she could see her trainer.

Looking into the whale's eye, Theresa saw something that frightened her. It made her feel things she hadn't felt in a long time. She shook them off and backed further up onto the stage. But the memories kept coming back. It was as if Katy were forcing her to remember.

Years ago, as a child, Theresa had been terribly shy. Playing by herself every day, she created her own special world where the sky changed colors according to people's moods, and dogs and cats could run for president if they wanted.

In Theresa's world, animals adopted people.

"Where would I sleep?" a cat might ask, giving the highest ratings to humans who said, "Why, anywhere. It would be your house, too."

"And the furniture?"

"Think of it as your personal scratching post."

"Excellent."

But then Theresa had gone to elementary school, where the teacher kept telling her that the sky was blue and that dogs belonged in the doghouse, not in the den reading a newspaper. Soon, she began to learn all sorts of "important" facts, like her multiplication tables and all the state capitals, and there was less and less time to think about holidays (on Theresa's calendar there were one hundred and eighty-two) or special sleds that worked on stairway banisters.

More and more, Theresa became like the average, quiet little girl that everyone expected her to be. But her special world did not go away. It just got buried under a sea of facts. It wasn't until she had a summer job at Ocean Park in California that her inner world came back. One morning, she had been sent down to sweep up the stadium before a big show. The park hadn't opened yet. All she could hear were the sprinklers jetting water, and the sea lions barking and playing in the cool early morning. When she came around to the side of the tank, there was Katy, who had been captured only a few months before, swimming over to her.

At first, Theresa had backed away. She knew that anyone caught playing with the whale would be fired immediately. But Katy raised her head out of the water and began to vocalize. It was then that Theresa's buried world came flooding back to her. She felt dizzy and pressed her forehead against the cool tank wall.

She saw Katy as part of her world, and they were having the most interesting conversation. Katy was telling her what it was like to swallow your food whole and rub your belly on the bottom of the ocean.

Theresa had shaken her head. Animals didn't talk to humans. She must have had too much coffee on an empty stomach. How could a whale and a woman be friends? But she had found a way to stay near Katy, to take care of her.

Now she said defensively, "That's just what I've done." Katy dove beneath the surface and Theresa watched her. She looked up to see an elderly gentleman approach from the back of the stadium.

When he came up to the other side of the tank,

Katy swam over to him, vocalizing for the first time in a week.

"Who are you?" Theresa asked him.

"I'm Joe Roberts, Derek Simpson's grandfather."

"Your grandson is here too, isn't he?" Theresa asked, glancing around the empty stadium.

"No, ma'am. He knows he's not allowed in the park anymore. No, I'm here on business." Joe held out the Indian carving that Derek had shown her earlier. "Would you mind having it appraised?" he asked her. "Derek could use the money."

"Sure, I guess so," Theresa said, wondering if there were some trick in it all. Then she remembered that the grandfather had been as surprised by Derek's behavior as she had.

"But on one condition," she added. "You'll have to be the one to pick it up. Derek's not allowed into the park under any circumstances." She walked down to the platform at the edge of the pool.

"Yes, I understand," said Joe, handing her the small carving, carefully wrapped up in a white handkerchief. "Thank you kindly."

He tipped his hat to her. "See you later, S'gana," he said, half waving and half saluting to the whale, who chattered back to him in her own language.

"I don't know what's going on around here,"

Theresa said to Katy, as she unwrapped the carving and turned the little whale over and over in her palm. It occurred to her that maybe she didn't want to know, that maybe knowing would change her life forever.

On his way out of the park, Joe passed Mr. Beaman, who was heading out to investigate a complaint about one of his food vendors.

"You're that . . . Derek's grandfather, aren't you?"

"Joe Roberts."

Mr. Beaman peeled off a pair of gloves he had brought along for the inspection. "If you knew the trouble that performance has given me," he said. "Parks everywhere wanting Derek for guest spots, wanting him to train other child trainers. Mr. Carpenter wants to fly him to California."

"I'm sorry for the . . ." Joe began.

"What are you doing here, anyway?" Mr. Beaman asked. Joe tried to explain, but he could tell that Mr. Beaman wasn't listening. "Tell you what, Joe. I'm going to have the cashier give you back your money." Mr. Beaman looked around quickly to make sure that no one else would hear what he was going to say next. "Then please, don't come back again."

"But, Mr. Beaman . . ."

"I don't care what it is—call it instinct," Mr. Beaman said, propelling Joe in the direction of the front gate.

"Something in my gut tells me to stay away from all of you."

Theresa couldn't stop thinking about what had happened that afternoon. She sat in her apartment drinking hot tea, even though it was ninety degrees out, and staring at the small whale carving she had set on the coffee table in front of her.

What was the carver thinking? The whale looked powerful and frightening, but also very graceful. What was it like to come upon a whale in the ocean? Up until that afternoon, Theresa had never feared killer whales.

But Theresa also knew if she let herself return to that young girl inside, she could understand Katy better. She closed her eyes and imagined herself as an Indian living long ago, watching the whales dive in search of fish, their powerful tail fins slapping the water. Then they rose like small islands all around her fishing boat, and she jumped into the water to play with them.

Theresa picked up the little carving from the table and looked at it closely. She traced all the patterns on its back and tail. She even traced the patterns of its teeth. Then she set it down in her lap and closed her eyes again.

In her sleep, she dreamed she was a whale, cutting

through the cold water, side by side, with her mate. Calling to each other in their high-pitched voices, they rolled and dove in the calm bay. Then she listened to them spout in unison. But as they headed for the mouth of the bay, the scene changed, and she was Theresa again, looking at Katy alone in her pool, breathing slowly, missing her home.

When Theresa awoke, she dressed as quickly as she could. The clock said 9:00 P.M. It was a short drive to Ocean Park. She stopped at the security entrance and flashed her badge.

"Nothing wrong I hope, Miss Summers," asked the security guard.

"No, I just forgot to give Katy her vitamins." Theresa smiled into his flashlight, then drove to the back parking lot near the whale stadium. She stood quietly at the back of the stadium and listened to Katy's breathing. The soft whoosh of Katy's breath, so far from anything like her home, was the saddest sound Theresa had ever heard. She wanted to run up and ask Katy to forgive her, but she couldn't. Not just yet.

For years, Katy had made Theresa feel special. Her job at Ocean Park was her whole life. And yet Theresa knew she no longer had any choice. She had to do what was right.

She went through the back door and quietly walked

onto the stage. Without a word, she slipped off her clothes and lowered herself into the water. For a moment, she treaded water, waiting for Katy to approach her. She had forgotten how wonderful it felt to go swimming without any clothes on. The cool water against her skin made her feel even closer to Katy. When Katy surfaced next to her, Theresa took hold of her friend's dorsal fin and they floated together for a moment.

"I'm so sorry, Katy," she whispered into the whale's back. "Please forgive me." Then came a reply that sounded more like water lapping against the side of a boat than a voice.

"My name," the voice said, "is S'gana."

If Theresa had looked up, she would have seen a young girl, her dark hair pushed behind her ears, dangling her legs in the water. But she kept her cheek pressed to the whale's back, and together they floated for what seemed like hours.

The morning after Joe dropped off the whale carving at Ocean Park, Derek received a call from Theresa, asking if she could come over.

"I think I know how much your carving's worth," was all she said. Disappointed, he hung up the phone.

"What if all she does is return it?" he asked Tani and Joe.

When Theresa arrived, Derek introduced her to Tani, and the three of them sat down at the table on the back porch while Joe fixed four glasses of mint tea with honey. Theresa pulled the carving out of her purse and set it in the center of the table.

"I wouldn't sell it," she said. "It's priceless."

"How priceless?" Joe asked.

"It's got the power to change a person's mind," Theresa said, wiping up the water ring her glass had left on the table. "To show her when she's done the wrong thing." She looked at Derek. "To make her want to right it."

"Good," was all Derek said, but underneath the table his feet tapped the floor in thanks.

Each person seated at the table had been transformed by the little whale, and so when Theresa said she was ready, Tani, Joe, and Derek all knew what that meant.

"What do we do now?" Theresa asked, and the three adults all looked at Derek. It made him feel very important to be the one everyone was turning to. Derek had dreamed about the moment when he no longer had to fight against those closest to him.

"I don't know," he said, and everyone laughed.

"Let's take a look at the way things stand," said Joe quietly, breaking the silence. "Our goal is to set S'gana free." He began jotting notes on the back of a napkin with a pen he had pulled from his shirt pocket. "That means we've got to steal her from Ocean Park, get her to the ocean . . ."

"Find her family . . ." Derek interrupted.

"Find her family," Joe scribbled down. At once, Theresa, Derek, and Tani realized how impossible it all sounded. How do you steal a whale? How would they get a plane to transport her? How would they find her mate? Joe must have been too busy scribbling, because he just kept on going.

"The first logical thing to do is figure out a way to steal her."

"Excuse me, Joe, but I'm not interested in going to jail," Tani said.

"Well, they're not going to just give her to us, are they?" Joe seemed to be getting a little exasperated with the whole group.

"Maybe they would," Theresa said, "under the right conditions."

"And what conditions might those be?" Joe asked.

"Maybe we could get them to fire her, sort of."

Joe chuckled at this, but Derek scooted around in his seat to face her.

"Go on, Theresa," Tani said.

"Well, in a way, S'gana is like an employee,"

Theresa said. "She eats a hundred and fifty pounds of fish a day when she's not depressed. That's worth a lot of money right there. What if we just got her to stop doing her job? Then maybe they'd want to get rid of her."

"That's just what we were going to do," Derek said, "but we never got that far."

"I'm not so sure." Tani got up. She poured them all another glass of tea and passed around the honey. "Zoos are full of animals that don't perform tricks, and people still go just to look at them. And didn't you tell us, Derek, that they gave S'gana shots when she didn't eat?"

"Yes, I'm afraid that's true," said Theresa, looking miserable.

"So they'd just give her some kind of drugs to make her more lively, wouldn't they?" Joe asked.

"It's possible."

They were all quiet for a minute, trying to think of some other reason Ocean Park would want to get rid of its star attraction.

"Maybe we should try to get people to stop coming to the park," Derek said, picking up the whale carving.

"But trying to change the people in this county one by one could take years," Joe argued. "S'gana hasn't got that kind of time." Everyone nodded. There was another long silence.

"Well, why do people go to Ocean Park?" Derek asked them. "They go for their kids, that's why. If we can get the kids to stop wanting to go, we won't have to worry about the adults."

"And children will be more sympathetic to S'gana anyway," Tani added.

"You forget, we're still talking about hundreds, even thousands of children," Joe said.

"Maybe we don't have to do it one by one," Theresa said. "If we did it at the right show, we could appeal to hundreds of children at one time."

"A whale show?" Tani asked.

"Derek and I can't even get near that park anymore," Joe said. But something about Theresa's idea just seemed right. Suddenly, their thoughts changed from how it all couldn't work to how it *could.*

"Not looking like that, you can't," Tani said.

"Do you think S'gana would recognize me if I went in a costume?" Derek asked.

"From what you tell me, she can do a lot more difficult things than that." Tani took hold of Derek's arm and squeezed. It seemed like they had a plan.

"But we've got to convince S'gana to stay in her body," said Theresa, taking the whale carving from Derek. "She may have a strong spirit, but her body's gotten weaker and weaker these last few weeks. If we do succeed in getting Ocean Park to let her go, she'll need all her strength for a cross-country trip."

"Now that she knows we're working to save her, I think she'll get better fast." But Derek didn't like the idea of not being able to talk to S'gana as a girl.

They joined hands.

"Then it's settled," Derek said. "We'll make an appeal to the children." He stood up. "Thank you for helping."

"Thank you," Joe answered, "for showing us how."

Nine

Old Dogs, New Tricks

Derek, Tani, Theresa, and Joe promised each other that they would work as quickly as they could, knowing how precious time was for S'gana. The first thing Joe did was call Clem and ask to meet him down at the toy shop. "I want to take your place at work Saturday, Clem," Joe said.

"As Katy the Killer Whale? Why would you want to do a thing like that?" Clem looped his thumbs under his suspenders and rocked back on his heels, as if waiting for a good long story.

"I'm thinking of applying there myself is all. And I'd like to know how it feels."

Clem rocked on. "You're not thinking of doing anything I wouldn't do, are you?" He picked up a newly painted caboose and shined the finish with his cuff.

"I can't think of anything you wouldn't do, Clem." Both men smiled, remembering their younger days.

"What the heck," said Clem, digging into his pocket. "I'm not partial to spending my retirement in that fuzzy inferno anyway." He tossed his employee identification card to Joe and explained how employees entered the park.

That same day, Tani took Derek down to the Ladies' Auxiliary Thrift Shop.

"I don't want to go as a girl, Tani," Derek complained, as they combed through rack after rack of dresses.

"They'll be watching for a little boy," Tani explained for the hundredth time. Derek stood silently as she held dresses up against him to test for the fit.

The day after Theresa went to see Tani, Derek, and Joe, she spoke to S'gana in her pool at the whale stadium.

"I know I could see you now if you appeared to me in your human form. And I'd like to see you once before you go. But it's important that you stay in your body as much as possible. You've got to make it strong again." She emptied the freezer of salmon and fed all of it to S'gana over the next few days.

It fell to Theresa to find out just where they were

going to take S'gana once they got her released. Tani insisted they plan for this stage.

The first thing Theresa needed was the records showing exactly where S'gana had been captured. These were fairly easy to obtain. She simply told the Ocean Park officials that she and Doc Barnes were interested in supplementing Katy's diet with indigenous fish.

Finding S'gana's pod was a long shot, but that didn't keep Theresa from trying. She made repeated telephone calls and visits to the university library in Madison that week. She read every book and journal article on orcas she could find. It was only then that she realized how little anyone knew about *Orcinus orca,* S'gana's species. The journals disagreed on everything from how much orcas needed to eat and sleep to whether fasting was a normal activity for them. She became more and more convinced that S'gana and other captive orcas were being used not only for profit, but for experimental purposes. Scientists wanted to see if they could get whales to survive and breed in captivity. But where was the concern for their quality of life? What she learned made her even more certain they were doing the right thing in setting S'gana free.

It wasn't until Saturday morning, the day they

were to make their appeal, that she called Derek to tell him her most exciting discovery. "I met an amazing man over the phone yesterday. You're going to love him."

"Why's that?"

"It's hard to explain, but I think he's the missing ingredient we've been looking for. He's got fascinating stories to tell about how orcas saved a sailor from being eaten by sharks and how one rescued a dog from drowning."

"Where does he live?"

"Potlatch Island, near Eagle Cove, off the coast of Canada. He studies orcas in the wild. He thinks he remembers S'gana being taken and wants her brought to his bay to wait for her pod."

"Is he Haida?"

"No. His name is Dr. Arvayo." Derek guessed that Eagle Cove was about three or four hundred miles north of his home in Port Espadon. He wondered how close that was to where Tani and her brother, Kwung, had grown up. Lately, he'd a hard time keeping Kwung out of his mind. Derek wondered whether he and his great-uncle shared the same spirit. If so, why did Ilyea make Kwung so rebellious? Would Derek start getting into fights as he got older? Would he shoot people?

Derek had several other questions for Theresa, but

they would have to wait. It was time to get ready.

"There's just one more thing," Theresa said. "Tell Joe that Dr. Arvayo is sending me a video of orcas in the wild, so he should be sure to bring the video projector."

"All right." Derek hung up. The video had been Joe's idea, and he insisted he could carry all the equipment, borrowed from the church, underneath his costume. Joe believed that once the audience saw orcas in their natural habitat, they would feel much more strongly about sending S'gana home. It bothered Derek that they couldn't test out this part of the plan; he told Tani that as she helped him dress.

"You do as much as you can, you leave the rest up to faith," she replied, bobby-pinning Derek's wig into place.

Then she left him and went downstairs to cook breakfast. Tani poured the orange juice. She cracked four eggs into a large bowl and whisked them. No one would have suspected that she was in any way nervous. But she was. There was Joe's health to worry about, with all the heat and the heavy equipment he would be carrying. Could they get arrested for what they were about to do? And what would her neighbors think? She was never one for a spectacle. Pouring the buttermilk into the biscuit mix, Tani beat the batter

until it was light and foamy. All these familiar movements comforted her. Tani knew that what they were
doing was the right thing, but she wanted to stay in
her normal routine as long as she could.

The drive to the park was a quiet one. Everyone
was concentrating. Joe was to go through the security
entrance, and Tani and Derek would wait together in
line. Once they had gotten in, they would bide their
time until the twelve o'clock show, which always had
the biggest crowds. They would not see Theresa until
it was all over.

When they arrived at the park, Joe left them at the
entrance and went through security the way Clem had
instructed him to do. He entered the narrow hall and
flashed Clem's ID at the officer, who was playing a
game of solitaire. The officer hardly looked up. Joe
noticed the name *Jim* on the man's identification
badge. Glancing at the long row of time cards made
Joe feel better. There were so many employees, he
could easily slip by unnoticed. He walked carefully,
trying to keep the equipment hidden beneath the folds
of his costume. He felt it was obvious that he was con-
cealing something, but the loose suit covered it well.

"Hold it a minute there, Clem."

He froze for a second, then mumbled, "I'm runnin'
late, Jim."

"This'll only take a second." Jim leaned over the counter and Joe turned around slowly. "Is it true that Jensen is selling off two hundred head? Heard it on the farm report this morning."

"Don't know."

"I was just wondering if he was in trouble is all. I mean with the drought and the crop failures . . ."

Joe shrugged his shoulders and turned around, carefully putting one foot in front of the other. Jim let it rest there, and Joe walked out onto the park side of security. He put the video equipment inside Clem's locker and went out to take his place greeting guests at the park entrance.

When Derek reached the ticket booth, he saw his photograph taped to the window, but the ticket seller hardly glanced at him. The hot, dry air that brushed past him and into her booth seemed to make her drowsy and unconcerned. Derek focused on the children around him. He watched the little girls, their skirts swinging behind them as they ran, and realized, in one panic-stricken moment, that he was wearing a skirt, too.

He tried to look at the clothing the way S'gana would. It was a lot easier to run in a dress, he thought. But the patent leather shoes were impractical. Derek found that he slipped on almost everything.

Derek tugged on his hair to make sure it was straight and went through the turnstile into the park. He looked for Joe but couldn't find him among the other costumed animals, so he decided to walk to the back of the park.

He took a seat on a bench facing the back of the whale stadium, and tried to focus on anything but the possibility that today they might not succeed. Soon, the crowd was streaming out. The first whale show was over. Among all the unfamiliar faces, Derek saw S'gana.

She wore a deep blue dress, the color of the ocean on a sunny day, and her sandals were the color of shells that had washed up on the beach long ago. Her hair was loose from its braid and tucked behind one ear. S'gana covered her mouth with her hand as if trying to stifle a giggle, then she held out her hand to him and he stood up. It felt natural, holding hands like that with a girl, and he wondered for a moment if that was because he himself was dressed like a girl.

"I've got only ten more minutes until I have to meet my grandfather," Derek told her as they walked toward the Oriental Garden, S'gana's favorite place.

"Human time is one thing I won't miss when I've returned," S'gana said. "You have pieces of time so small that no one can really do anything with them.

What can you do at 12:57?"

S'gana watched a woman go by in a Japanese kimono. She had a flower tucked behind one ear. S'gana reached down and plucked a camellia blossom from the bush at her side, stopping in the middle of the path to fix it behind her ear.

"There are only three kinds of time in the ocean," she said, showing off her new adornment. "Time to eat, time to play, time to rest. We never stop to look at little timekeepers and say, 'Goodness, it's noon. Time to eat.'

"Here," she continued, "it is always time for something I'd rather not do when I'm doing something I'd rather do."

"Like listening to Peter's flute?"

"Yes," she said wistfully. "His flute reminds me of my brothers in the sea . . . I think you call them the humpback whales. Do you know who I mean?"

Derek confessed that he'd only seen them in pictures. He'd never heard them sing.

They picked out a bench off in a corner, the scents of rose and honeysuckle surrounding them. Peter Montgomery was nowhere to be seen. For once, Derek was glad. He wanted S'gana all to himself today. They sat quietly for a while.

"Sometimes, I'm scared of liking things too much,"

he said. "Because I know they may not last." He wanted to go on, but it all seemed so complicated.

S'gana looked at him curiously. "What an odd thing to say."

She broke another long silence with a sigh. "It is easy to get to know a whale. It is hard to get to know a boy."

Though he wanted to disagree with her, Derek found that he couldn't. He didn't understand himself just then.

"Has Theresa told you our plan?" he asked, to change the subject.

"Yes." S'gana pulled the blossom from her hair and twirled it between her fingers. "I know it will be our last chance."

Derek almost looked at his watch but stopped himself. "S'gana, why do you think I don't get those feelings of being laughed at by Ilyea anymore?"

"Why?" S'gana seemed to give that serious thought. "You and Ilyea are not two separate selves anymore," she said finally. "You work together now."

Derek stood up. The answer gave him confidence. "I'm scared," he said, "but I know our plan will work. It's just got to. I have to go now. At least promise me that you'll take care of your body so it will be ready for that long trip."

"The spirit needs to be taken care of, too," S'gana told him. "Right now, it is only the time spent with you and listening to Peter's flute that gives me rest." S'gana hugged him tightly. "Good-bye. It may be a long time before we see each other again." She smiled as she backed away from him and disappeared.

Derek stood there for a moment after she'd left. He wasn't sure which had made him feel better—what she'd said about spending time with him or how she'd hugged him, as if that were the most natural thing in the world.

He hurried across the park to the pinniped exhibit and found his costumed grandfather sitting on a bench in the shade, sipping lemonade through a long straw.

"Joe, didn't it say in Clem's handbook that the costumed characters aren't supposed to sit down or eat on the job?"

"Yes," Joe answered, from between the teeth of Katy's wide grin. He didn't make any effort to move.

"Well, get up then," Derek said. "You're going to get fired and ruin our whole plan."

"Don't worry, son," Joe said. "I'm just a little hot, that's all." Derek couldn't understand why Joe would jeopardize their whole plan to save S'gana just because he was a little hot. He looked around nervously, half expecting to see Mr. Beaman come around the corner at any time. Finally, when Derek thought he couldn't wait any longer, his grandpa pushed himself up off the bench.

"Just needed a little rest. I'm good as new." Derek took hold of one of Joe's fins. He'd feel better when his grandpa was out of this stupid costume. Hadn't Clem said it was twenty degrees hotter in there?

Joe pushed his grandson in the direction of the whale stadium. "Now, go. You do your job and I'll do mine." Derek took a last look at Joe through the mouth of the whale costume, then turned and walked away slowly. "You'll see. This old dog still has a few tricks up his sleeve," Joe called after him.

After Derek left, Joe began to feel the heat again. The sweat from his forehead rolled down and stung his eyes. He shot some water from the drinking fountain between the teeth of his costume into his mouth and tried to linger for a while in the shade.

Suddenly, he felt cooled by a stiff breeze. He turned to see a young girl approaching him. Her long, dark hair was pushed back over the shoulders of a blue dress. She smiled at him, not so much with her mouth as with her narrowed eyes, and he smiled back.

"You have my daughter Wiba's smile," Joe said as she came near and took his hand.

"I appear to you in her body," she answered. For a

moment, Joe felt a keen sense of regret.

"Thank you, Joe." S'gana hugged him. "Thank you for giving me hope." Then she turned and disappeared down the path that led to the whale stadium.

Theresa had arrived early and gotten ready before the crowd collected. First, she locked and barricaded the door that led backstage and to her dressing room so that no one would be able to get in once the show had started. Using a can of vegetable shortening, she smeared a wide swath on each side of the platform. Even if someone were able to leap over the retaining wall, they would have a devil of a time reaching her or any of the video equipment.

Then she sat down to say a private goodbye to S'gana.

"I know I shouldn't talk like this . . ." she began. S'gana swam over to her and stuck out her tongue for Theresa to rub. "It's possible that something could go wrong today, and I just want you to know how I feel if it does and I'm never allowed to see you again." S'gana backed away from Theresa and swam to the far end of the tank, as if she refused to hear that kind of talk.

"First of all, I've known you were unhappy for a long time, but I needed you too much to do anything about it." Theresa got up and began walking along the small space she had provided for herself and the film equipment.

"I guess you could say that I needed you more than I loved you. I stopped thinking about what was best for you. Or maybe I never knew." It was hard to tell if S'gana was listening, she seemed so still. "And even though it's been hard on you, you really changed my life, S'gana. I'll never forget you."

"You'll never have to." Theresa turned toward the voice that spoke to her. A young girl in a dark blue dress and cream-colored sandals was perched on the slide-out platform. Derek had described S'gana's broad cheeks and dark skin, but Theresa still couldn't believe her eyes. She went over all the different ways the young girl could have gotten in. But then she glanced at the whale, who was once again in that peculiar trance she had been in whenever Derek was around.

"You're who I think you are, aren't you?"

"Yes. We don't have to be parted, you and I."

"I don't understand."

"There was a time and a place when whales and humans lived together. It can be that way again."

Theresa shook her head. Not in this world. Not anymore.

S'gana explained. "Hundreds of years ago, a Haida

boy became a man by running across the back of a black whale." She tossed her hair and laughed. "They thought by keeping their paddles in the water, they could sneak up on us. We didn't need to hear them. We could sense their fear. But it was important that their boys became men. And that we helped them."

Theresa walked over to S'gana and touched her shoulder. She ran a finger across the girl's wide cheek. She wanted to say something, but there were no words for what she wanted to say. She pressed her face into S'gana's hair and stroked it.

"Now, you are a woman," S'gana said, "and soon, I will be a whale again." Gently, S'gana separated herself from Theresa and dove into the water.

Tani wandered through the park, trying to admire Peter's flowers, but she felt restless. She wanted to help, too, but her only job was to troubleshoot, and it just wasn't enough for her. Once Tani was in on something, she wanted to be in on it all the way.

That's when she thought of her own plan. She believed in the children, but it was the grown-ups who paid for the tickets. And try as she might, she didn't think anyone she knew in Sutton County would believe the story about S'gana. They had been adults for too long and had forgotten how to believe in such things. Tani thought that if she could find a way to make it personal to them, to tie the whale's plight to their own, they might be more responsive.

It was a plan that involved a lie, or maybe not really a lie. At the time, Tani comforted herself by saying, "I'm doing the wrong thing. But I'm doing it for the right reasons." She looked around the crowd for someone she knew, and spotted Clara Brinkman sitting just three rows from the back. Something of a busybody, Clara seemed like the perfect choice. Tani slid in next to her.

"Well hello, Tani," Clara said, anxious to get in some conversation before the program started.

"Have you heard the rumor about this whale?" Tani began, as soon as Clara tapered off.

"Of course," Clara said. She always pretended to know what was going on. Otherwise she would lose her reputation as the source of all information. "What do you make of it?" she asked slyly.

"Well, I, for one, don't know if I believe it. But then again . . ."

"Why not?" Clara was truly interested now. A rumor was nice, but a controversial one was even more intriguing.

"Do you remember it stopped raining in Sutton County right around the time this park opened? Well, whales are highly sensitive and intelligent creatures, or so I've heard. They even get stomach ulcers when they're depressed."

"What *are* you talking about?" Clara asked. Clearly whales were not high on her list of subjects for conversation.

"Well, that this whale's being captive here is causing the drought."

"That is remarkable," said Clara, though on the whole she looked disappointed.

"Whales are mysterious creatures," Tani said, excusing herself and walking away.

A good farmer never plants just one seed. Tani planted several seeds throughout the audience that day. The stories were all slightly different, but the message was the same: *keeping this whale captive is causing our drought.* There were those who dismissed it entirely. But farmers rely heavily on Mother Nature, so the rumor made more than one good man or woman of Sutton County uneasy.

Just before the show began, Tani was resting in an aisle seat, trying to decide if she should approach one more person about the "rumor" she had heard, when she felt a tap on her shoulder.

"Do you think it will work?"

The girl in the next seat took Tani's hand and

looked up into her eyes. Tani stroked the girl's soft hands between her own calloused ones.

"Sometimes love is not enough," she told the girl.

"But love is a powerful force," S'gana responded.

"I know, dear." Tani put her arm around S'gana and held her until the introductory music began.

Joe's exhaustion made Derek realize how chancy their plan was. Any one of them might get caught before they had finished what they had to do. And even if they were successful, and the audience heard what they had to say, would they care? As Derek walked back toward the whale stadium, he tried to think about anything but the possibility that they might fail. He entered from the back, walked halfway down, and sat just one seat from the main aisle.

"Excuse me, sir," he said, stepping over the knees of the man in the aisle seat. Try as he might, he could not imitate the way girls talked. He settled into his seat and waited for the program to begin.

The audience was restless with the waiting and the heat. The women fanned themselves with paper plates and old envelopes they found in their purses. Most of the men had handkerchiefs out and swabbed at their foreheads.

When the music began, everyone sat a little

straighter and quieted down. Derek didn't know why the music stirred him so, and why the sight of S'gana doing her first leaps and dives gave him goose bumps. He thought the act would make him feel sad, knowing what he did. Instead, he looked forward to it.

He could see that the audience was getting what they had hoped for as well—a chance to forget their own troubles and watch S'gana gracefully execute one move after the other. Theresa and S'gana moved together differently now, Derek thought as he watched them. They performed like partners. The audience must have sensed it, too. Derek heard the comments all around.

"Look at the way that bit of a girl handles that huge whale," said a woman one row down from him. "She doesn't seem the least bit afraid of him."

"It's not a him, Mother, it's a her."

"What difference does it make?" the woman snapped back at her child.

The exchange brought the fear back to Derek. What if they ignored his plea, booed at him, told him to get on with the show? He tried to block those thoughts from his mind and remember that he was speaking to the children. He held onto the hope that they would understand. They had to.

Ten

The Kidcott

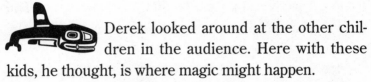Derek looked around at the other children in the audience. Here with these kids, he thought, is where magic might happen.

He saw Mr. Beaman come in with his wife and children and seat themselves just beyond the water zone. Derek glanced over at the boy, about his own age, and the little girl holding her mother's hand, and felt a little better.

Reaching into the pocket of his dress, Derek pulled out the little whale carving and turned it over in his hand. Time after time, the little carving had shown people that S'gana needed their help. But Derek knew its magic worked best on those who held it, so as he sat waiting for Theresa to give him his signal, he began to pass the carving around.

"Look at this," he said to the child next to him. "It's a carving of a black whale just like the one you've been watching."

"Oooh, it looks mean." But she took it in her hand and began tracing the smooth surface with her finger.

"It's not mean, it's powerful," Derek told her. "The artist who carved it wanted us to see how majestic she was and to respect the great whale."

"What does majestic mean?" the little girl asked.

"It means like a king," said her older brother, who took the whale from her hands and examined it closely.

"This is neat." He passed it on to a cousin who was visiting the park with the boy's family that day. Derek watched the whale move farther and farther from him and breathed a sigh of relief. He would leave it in the audience to work its magic. He turned his attention to the stage.

Something was wrong. Theresa was supposed to set up the VCR during the intermission, but there was no equipment on the stage. Where was Joe?

Derek saw Theresa searching the audience. For some reason, Joe hadn't made it. Derek's first thought was that he had to go look for his grandfather, but S'gana's words rang in his ears: "I know this will be our last chance." Slipping off his shoes, he excused himself to the man next to him. He couldn't wait any longer.

Derek's skirt stuck to his legs as he ran down the steps toward the tank, trying to gain speed for the jump. When he got there, he leaped, planting his feet halfway up the wall, but the slippery surface made him lose his footing.

"Oh, my God, look at that little girl!" someone shouted, as Derek tried to pull himself up.

"Jim, Rick, get that kid!" Mr. Beaman shouted. It was the last thing Derek heard before slapping hard against the water.

For a moment, he didn't know where he was. Then, as if in a dream, Derek sensed S'gana near him. She was so huge she seemed to surround him at once, but he wasn't afraid. He put his hands out and felt the smoothness of her skin.

Then S'gana was underneath him and lifting him above the surface of the water. As he struggled to push down his skirt, Derek realized that he had lost his wig. Suddenly he was aware of the audience in front of him. They seemed torn between laughter and fear, wondering if this was all part of the show.

"It's that kid again," shouted Mr. Beaman. "I want him out of that pool!"

S'gana swam over to the platform, where Theresa was waiting with a bullhorn. She handed it to Derek.

"We'll save the video for last," she said, giving him a thumbs-up sign.

"All right." He patted S'gana's great back and returned to the middle of the pool. Then, carefully, he stood up, rocking a little to get used to the sleekness of her body. He'd practiced a speech, but now he couldn't remember a thing. He stared out at the packed audience, amazed. They seemed to be waiting patiently for what would come next.

Mr. Beaman, however, was not so calm. Derek saw the director gesturing wildly toward the pool, but the security guards weren't about to jump in with a killer whale. Out of the corner of his eye, he saw them trying to figure out a way to get onto the stage. He turned on the bullhorn.

"The first thing I want to tell everyone is that I'm not a girl." This caused a wave of laughter from the audience. Derek blushed, realizing that since he had lost his wig, this fact must be pretty obvious. He rubbed his head.

"I guess you knew that." Another peal of laughter from the audience. "What I have to tell you is very important," he continued. "I've come here to talk to the children. You are the ones who can help my friend S'gana, the black whale."

Derek heard Mr. Beaman yell something to his

security guards, and turned to see the director hoisting himself over the tank wall. Mr. Beaman stepped onto the greased part of the stage and, after several comical attempts at keeping his balance, fell into the pool. As he thrashed around, trying to get out, S'gana sank deeper into the water, and started to swim toward him. Derek grabbed her dorsal fin and sat down quickly, straddling her back. Mr. Beaman's eyes grew wide at the sight of her open mouth and rows and rows of teeth. With her big head, S'gana lifted him out of the water far enough so that the security guards could grab his arms, then swam serenely back to the center of the pool to the accompanying applause of the audience. Derek tried to remember where he'd left off, but he couldn't.

"Whales see by using something called echolocation," he said in a sudden burst of inspiration. "They send out radar from their foreheads and it bounces off everything—the sand, the other fish, the ocean reefs. Look at this pool!" he shouted, but the feedback from the bullhorn made him lower his voice again. "These smooth walls are like a house of mirrors. Everywhere she looks, it's the same picture. It would make me crazy." Derek tried to gauge the audience's reaction, but it was impossible. They were listening patiently, waiting, he thought, for his point.

"We know what it feels like to be sad," Derek

continued. "But S'gana is so sad that if she's kept here, she'll die of a broken heart." As he tried to think of something else to say, Derek's attention was drawn to the entrance of the stadium.

A man in a killer whale costume was making his way along the tank passing out stuffed animals, likenesses of Katy, to the children in the front row. Though his large plastic bag looked like it was full of the toys, Derek could see that it was knotted about halfway down. Mr. Beaman ran up to the costumed figure and patted him on the back, glad to have someone diverting attention away from Derek and S'gana. The whale handed Mr. Beaman a plush toy and brushed his face with one flipper.

Suddenly, he flung the rest of the bag into the pool, and Derek watched as it floated among the toy animals that scattered across the water's surface. Running to the far side of the tank, the costumed whale pulled off its head and tossed it into the audience.

"Joe!" Theresa shouted.

Quickly, Joe unzipped the rest of his suit and stepped out of it. He had made it as far onto the stage as Mr. Beaman had, but instead of fighting to keep his balance, he held his nose and slid right in. Soon, he was swimming the breast stroke out to S'gana. With Derek's help, he crawled up on the whale and sat on her back, holding her dorsal fin from the other side.

S'gana closed her mouth gently around the bag of video equipment and delivered it to Theresa. Soon, the video was rolling and, for a moment, even Derek watched it. It was a glorious sight. A pod of black whales frolicked in a calm bay, skimming over the surface, then diving and leaping far out of the water. As their great bodies crashed back into the sea, a spray of water covered the wall where the image was projected. Derek turned to face the audience.

"That was S'gana's home before she was captured to perform tricks for us here at Ocean Park. Once, I was just like you! I enjoyed the show. I didn't think about where she might have come from or that she was taken away from her family and her friends."

There was so much more to say, but something told Derek to be silent. He felt a stirring in the audience. S'gana sighed beneath him, sending up a mist of water. He sat down to rub her. Gently, he ran his hands along her flanks and down her perfectly curved forehead. Joe, too, was rubbing her dorsal fin and the sensitive area around her blowhole. When he looked up, Derek saw that no one had moved. Several of the children were watching them closely, but the adults looked around uncomfortably. Derek felt that he knew these children, that he could read their minds.

"I knew that if I told you, you would help her," Derek said, standing up again and addressing the children. "S'gana wants to go home!"

"What can *we* do?" shouted the boy who had first held Derek's whale carving. "It's not like we put her there."

"No," Derek shouted back. "But you're helping to keep her here by coming to the park. What we need is a boycott. That's when you stop doing something as a form of protest. But in this case, we need boys and girls. A kidcott! Kids have to stop coming to Ocean Park."

"But that's not enough," Joe said. His voice couldn't carry very far, so Derek handed him the bullhorn. "You've got to write letters—to the TV stations, to the newspapers, to Washington, D.C." Theresa spoke into the microphone on stage: "Children, help your parents understand, as Derek has helped us. I love this whale, but it's time to set her free."

"Let's help her get back where she came from," Derek said, pointing to the screen. "You can start by leaving the stadium now. Tell your parents you'll meet them at the car, but go, go, go!"

Slowly, it began happening. The children who had touched the whale carving were the first to go. The adults were still confused. They wanted someone with authority to speak. But the children's minds were clear. They understood what had to be done and they were prepared to do it. Their parents argued, pleaded, threatened.

"I'll fix your favorite supper."

"You'll have no television privileges for a week."

"You've just lost your allowance, young lady."

But the children left anyway. A young boy ran up to the tank and tossed Derek's whale carving back to him.

"What's your name again?" he said.

"Derek."

"I'm Sam Beaman. See you around, Derek."

"Sam!" Derek heard the boy's father call. "You're benched for the season." But Sam just ran up the steps past his parents and out into the park. The little girl tried to follow her brother, but Mrs. Beaman kept a firm grip on the struggling child as her husband rushed off after their son.

When the children had all gone, the parents looked at one another. What were they to do now? Some followed their children, but many of them stayed behind. Soon they were shouting questions at Joe. Why had he gotten involved? Was the whale really unhappy? She didn't look so bad. Finally, someone shouted out what was on many of their minds: "You think this has anything to do with the drought?"

"I don't know," Joe said. "Maybe it does."

They shook their heads and muttered among themselves. Slowly they filed out to find their children, and to make their own sense of what had happened. Soon, the stadium was empty, except for Tani.

Derek, Theresa, and Joe said good-bye to S'gana. She lifted her body out of the water for a hug from all three of them. Mr. Beaman, his security guards, and a small crowd of onlookers were waiting for them when they came out.

"I'm not sure which one of you called me," said a man holding a microphone, "but I'm grateful." Next to him, a woman with a video camera on her shoulder started filming them, to the great irritation of Mr. Beaman.

Another woman pushed a microphone into Mr. Beaman's face. "I'm Alexandra Pratt from the *Sentinel Star.* Do you have any comments?"

"No," Mr. Beaman said firmly, waving them away.

"First, I want to talk to *them,*" he told the guards who had surrounded Theresa, Derek, and Joe as they climbed over the tank wall. "Then I'm going to turn them over to the sheriff."

"May I come, too?" Tani asked, coming up behind Mr. Beaman.

"Who are *you*?" Mr. Beaman looked as though he couldn't take anymore.

"I'm his wife, and his grandmother." Tani said, pointing to Joe and to Derek.

"Why not? Maybe you can shed some light on this."

They sat in a row before the broad battleship of a desk in Mr. Beaman's office—Tani, Joe, Derek, and Theresa. Mr. Beaman told the guards to wait outside.

"What I'm trying to figure out here," he said, "is what's in this for all of you." He held a paperweight in his hand as if it were a hardboiled egg that he intended to crack.

"Are you being paid off by some competitor who wants to sabotage our enterprise here?" Mr Beaman demanded, tapping nervously on the edge of his desk. He homed in on Derek. "Just who are you working for?"

"I don't work for anyone, sir. I'm just a kid."

"A kid?" Mr. Beaman laughed. "Kids don't make trouble the way you do. How did you get Theresa to go in on this with you? What are you paying her?"

Theresa opened her mouth to protest, then everyone started talking at once. Derek told the story of S'gana, Joe wanted to know about the legal implications, Theresa explained what she had learned about orcas, and Tani requested a drink of water.

"That's enough!" Mr. Beaman shouted, and everyone stopped. "I'm going to give you each a chance to explain yourself and I want you to do it quickly. No interrupting. And stick to the facts."

But "the facts" to Derek were not the same as they were to a man like Mr. Beaman. They looked around at each other uneasily. Certainly Mr. Beaman wasn't going to change. They all tried to think of a way to explain things so he could understand. Tani began.

"I am a Haida Indian," she told Mr. Beaman, who nodded for her to go on. "In my culture, it is wrong to injure the black whale. Terrible consequences result. That's why I wanted to help free S'gana."

Mr. Beaman sighed and rubbed at his eyes. "Let's start there. Who is this S'gana again?"

No one said anything.

Derek swallowed. It was his turn. "Remember all those stories about the dolphin girl?" he asked Mr. Beaman.

"How did you know about that?" Mr. Beaman slapped his hand over a file on his desk. "That was strictly confidential." He glared at Theresa, as Derek tried to explain.

"Well, do you remember how children could see her but none of the adults could? And how all the children gave the same description? She wore a cape and a pointed hat and had long dark hair." Mr. Beaman nodded for Derek to continue. "Well, she was the whale's spirit, roaming the park."

Mr. Beaman sat back in his chair and twirled around to look out the window. Then he turned back to face them. They could see from the look on his face that he found Derek's explanation comical.

"Let me get this straight," he said. "Because the whale is unhappy and wants to return to the ocean, her spirit roams around the park in the form of a little girl who can only be seen by children . . ."

"It's not that she can only be seen by children," Tani interrupted him. "She can only be seen by those who believe in her existence. *I've* seen her."

"So have I," came a chorus of voices.

Mr. Beaman went on, unruffled, a smile playing on his lips. " . . . a little girl who can only be seen by children and lunatics? I suppose you all have lengthy conversations with this child?"

Theresa was growing irritated with the way Mr. Beaman was talking to them. "Look, Bob, if it's facts you want, then I'll give you facts. The same ones I had to face." She sat forward in her chair and ticked off the reasons on her fingers.

"First, everyone who saw a little girl at the scene of all the incidents described her in exactly the same way. Second, these incidents always coincided with times when Katy—S'gana, rather—would act as if she were drugged or in a trance and not respond to my commands. And third, it is a fact that whales do not live out their normal lifespans while in captivity. They are sensitive creatures of highly developed intelligence who were not meant to be captured and used by marine parks just for the entertainment and profit of human beings." Mr. Beaman started to respond. But Theresa was not finished.

"I, too, have to follow my conscience. You can't imagine how hard this is for me, Bob, because I love my job." She paused just long enough to take in another breath."But I'm telling you this, and you can ask Doc for her opinion, too, if you want. That whale is dying. It doesn't take a genius to figure it out. I can't be a party to that. I love her. And even if you don't care about her, think about what her death will mean to you. The publicity could put you out of business forever."

Mr. Beaman sat at his desk, each hand clasped around a corner, and took a deep breath. Then he looked at Joe. "Got anything to add?"

"Nothing that hasn't already been said."

He buzzed his outer office, and the security guards came in. "I'm through with everyone but Theresa," he said, and the rest of them filed out, each glancing back at her. When they were alone again, Mr. Beaman and

Theresa talked for some time.

"It's a damn shame, Theresa." Mr. Beaman shook his head slowly. "You were my best trainer. I'd say you were born to work with whales, and now you won't be able to get near a marine park."

"That's not the only place whales live, you know, Bob." She reached over the desk and touched his arm. Remembering what S'gana had told her, she said, "There was a time and a place when whales and humans lived together. It can be that way again." Then she stood back and waited for him to call the security guards.

But he hesitated. "They'll just catch another one if this one is set free, Theresa. Whales are worth a lot of money."

Theresa picked up the picture of Mr. Beaman's children from his desk and looked at it for a moment. "Then I'll just have to hope that you and 'they,' whoever they are, start learning from the children."

Theresa was escorted to the jail, where she and Joe were charged with disorderly conduct and disturbing the peace. Clem drove Tani and Derek over to bail them out, so everyone could go home.

In the car they were silent, wondering if they'd done the right thing. Even if they had, would it do any good? Or would the children simply go home and forget what had happened?

Eleven

An Owl in the Village

After they were released from the police station, Clem drove everyone back to the park to pick up their cars. Derek sat quietly between Joe and Theresa in the back seat, pulling on the cover of the ashtray in front of him and letting it snap back into place.

"I think this calls for a victory celebration," Joe said, and he invited them all to join him at the Hofbrau House.

"But Ocean Park hasn't decided to set S'gana free yet," Derek argued.

"We accomplished what we set out to do today," said Joe, putting his arm around his grandson, "and that was no easy feat."

Derek wondered what they'd call the celebration

when S'gana was set free. As tired as he was, now was the wrong time to let up. "So what do we do next?"

"Tonight, we rest . . ." Tani reached back and covered the ashtray with her hand. "And tomorrow we plan our next move." She invited Theresa to have dinner with them, but Theresa declined.

"I need to be by myself for a while," she said quietly, as they pulled into the employee parking lot. In all the excitement, Derek had forgotten that Theresa had lost her job. She had made the biggest sacrifice of all of them, giving up work she loved in order to set S'gana free.

Derek hugged her and said, "I know what you mean. I need some peace and quiet, too."

Joe laughed and put his arm around Tani. "Well, I need a noisy bar, and a couple of friends to tell my tall tales to."

At home, Tani fixed a cold supper tray filled with German rye, brick cheese, mustard, cucumbers, and the first tomatoes from the garden. Though the food looked delicious, most of it stayed on the plate. What little they ate, they ate in silence.

"Are you afraid for S'gana?" Derek asked Tani as they cleared away the dishes. But the phone rang before she could reply. Tani answered it, spoke for a minute, then pressed the receiver into her stomach.

"It's someone from the newspaper. Do you want to talk?" There was nothing that Derek wanted to do less. He started to shake his head no, but then realized this was the sort of attention they needed. He took the phone from Tani.

"Hello, Derek. This is Steven Kinney from the *Sentinel Star.* Mind if I ask you a couple of questions about what happened at Ocean Park today?"

"Okay."

"I guess the most obvious one is, why did you do it?"

"Because we're friends," was the first answer that occurred to Derek, but instead he used a line he'd been practicing with Theresa. "We want to see the whale reintroduced to the wild."

"Why is that so important?"

"Because she's not happy here. Would you be if you had to live like her?"

"I don't know. Free food and a free place to live doesn't sound too bad."

Derek thought about how angry S'gana would be if she heard that. "She already *had* free food and a free place to live." He was trying to be patient with the reporter, but at the moment, he was growing tired of how long it took some people to understand.

"I guess you have a point there," said Mr. Kinney,

laughing. "Do you have the backing of any wildlife organizations, or are you doing this on your own?"

"My grandma and grandpa are helping me, and Theresa Summers . . ."

"I've seen her show. Frankly, I can't figure out what she stands to gain from this. There aren't a lot of marine parks that will want to hire her now."

"All you can talk about is free food and jobs, but I'm talking about saving someone's life." Derek spoke quickly into the receiver. He wasn't supposed to be disrespectful to adults, but a lot of the rules he'd been living by seemed silly to him now, with S'gana's life at stake. "Kids know what's right sometimes more than adults do. Sometimes we see things you can't."

There was a long pause before Mr. Kinney said, "Don't get me wrong, Derek. I understand what you're saying." When they finished talking, Derek handed the phone over to Tani, who gave the reporter Theresa's phone number.

"What do you think is going to happen, Tani?" Derek asked his grandmother after she hung up.

"I don't know," she said, putting her arm around him. "Come on, let's play some checkers."

In bed that night, Derek looked up at the stars, taking comfort that it was the same sky for S'gana, his mother and father, Theresa, his friend Michael. All those he loved, near and far, had at least that in common.

The morning paper ran a front-page story with a picture of Derek and Joe atop S'gana's back shouting to the audience. *Local Group Demands Whale Be Freed,* said the headline. At breakfast, Joe read the story aloud.

"Threatening Ocean Park with a 'kidcott,' Derek Simpson, Joe Roberts, and Theresa Summers, the whale's trainer, asked children and adults alike to protest the captivity of Katy, Ocean Park's resident orca . . . It is unclear the extent to which this group, a grassroots organization of whale lovers, can carry out its threat." Joe put the paper down.

"I've got some ideas of what we might do at the county fair," he said. "Our booth should be a place where people can learn more about orcas and why we're working to return S'gana to the wild."

And so they began again. Derek was finding out what it meant to be an adult, and he wasn't at all sure that he liked it. He'd always felt that if you knew something was right, you just did it, and everything fell into place. Like the kidcott. But now Joe and Tani were talking about committees, petitions, letter-writing campaigns. All these things took time, no matter how hard they worked, and how much time did S'gana have?

A few days later, Theresa called to say that she'd heard Mr. Beaman was having trouble getting a new trainer for S'gana.

"It's a mixed blessing. I think it shows we're having some effect on the park, but it also means that S'gana won't have contact with anyone."

"I'm glad she's not performing for them anymore," Derek said, but he couldn't help thinking of S'gana with no one to play with, alone in her tank and losing hope.

"I think we should try to see her," he told Tani after he hung up.

Tani thought a minute. "I know it would do her good, but how? Ocean Park will never allow it."

"They want to keep her alive as much as we do," Derek said. "If she's depressed, she'll get sick more easily. Maybe we can convince Mr. Beaman to let us see her to cheer her up."

Tani gave Joe a look, but said nothing. Joe picked up one of the toy trains he had brought home from the shop, and carefully brushed sandpaper around the lip of its smokestack, giving the train his full attention.

Without looking up, he said, "It's worth a try."

Derek slid into the front seat next to Joe, leaving the door open as an invitation to Tani. There wasn't much room, but Derek liked it that way, one shoulder pressed against each grandparent. It reminded him of riding between his mother and father, a long time ago.

As Joe parked the car, Tani said, "I'll wait here until you know if we can see her."

"All right," Joe said, giving her a kiss.

As Joe and Derek approached the gate at Ocean Park, a security guard blocked their path.

"We're here to speak to Mr. Beaman," Joe said.

"I'm sorry, but my orders are to escort you off park property."

"We have important information about the whale's health that we have to relay to Mr. Beaman." Joe stood firmly planted on the asphalt path that led to the ticket booths. Derek turned away while the security guard thought it over. Through the iron gates, he could see the dense greenery that had first welcomed him to Ocean Park. The exotic birds stood out sharply on their perches, calmly preening their feathers.

"All right. We'll call from the security phone." The guard walked toward his office, and Joe followed him. Derek wandered over to the iron bars and peered inside.

"Say, aren't you the whale's friend?" A girl popped her head through the ticket booth window. "It's because of you I'm so bored, you know." She pushed her hair behind her ears and looked at him curiously.

"What do you mean?"

"All we get these days is out-of-towners. Most people from Sutton County won't come near the place. You should see the mail, too. I watched them unload a duffel bag this morning. Straight to Mr. Beaman's office."

"You mean people are really writing to him?"

"Kids are writing to him." She leaned farther out the window and said in a loud whisper, "I even wrote. Of course, I'm not a kid. I'm sixteen. You don't think that's a conflict of interest, do you?"

Derek didn't answer. On the other side of the fence, the parrots and the cockatoos had begun hopping up and down anxiously, but they could only rise a few inches on the strength of their clipped wings. Instinctively, Derek ducked at a shadow that passed above him. When he straightened up again, he saw a bird circling far above. It soared calmly overhead, slowly flapping its enormous steel-colored wings. The shadow grew longer as the bird dropped closer.

Joe came running over to join Derek. "What the . . . ?"

They both stared at the winged creature. Derek was suddenly afraid. It wasn't the bird, but something else he felt.

"What is it, Joe?" he asked.

"It's a great gray owl," Joe said softly, as if he didn't

believe it himself. "But they're not from around here. They come from farther north." The owl settled itself in a maple tree close to the edge of the park, and regarded the scene below indifferently. Derek could see its yellow eyes flash beneath its feathered brows.

"Why is an owl out during the day?" Derek asked.

"It was here yesterday, too," the ticket taker broke in. "It's driving the birdkeepers crazy."

Derek had trouble focusing on her words. "What about S'gana, Joe?"

"Well, Beaman won't let us in. But he did agree to play a tape of Peter's flute music for her. We'll stop by on the way home and ask Peter to make one."

"But how *is* she? Is S'gana all right?" Derek heard his voice getting louder.

Joe took hold of his grandson's shoulders. "Settle down, Derek."

But Derek couldn't settle down. Something was terribly wrong. He broke free and ran to find his grandmother.

Tani sat on a bench at the edge of the parking lot, staring at her folded hands. She didn't need him to explain what had happened. She had seen the owl.

"Tani, I know that bird is a sign." Derek stroked his grandmother's arm, then grasped her warm hands with his own chilled ones. "I want to understand. Please."

Her eyes met Derek's briefly before returning their gaze to her lap.

"Death," she said. "An owl in the village means death."

Derek stared at her for a moment, understanding more from her body, her stillness. He stood up. "No!"

"It's only a sign, Derek. A possibility." But even as Tani spoke the words, Derek knew that she didn't mean them.

The next few moments were blurred, just as they'd been when Derek ran down the steps to join S'gana in her tank. He wove through the small crowd outside the gate. The turnstile was easy to jump, and since the security guards were dealing with the birds, he was able to slip off unseen to the path that led to the whale stadium.

He ran so quickly that the people and things he passed looked like he was seeing them from the window of a fast-moving car. He cut behind the dolphin pool, staying away from the main path. Soon he heard voices behind him, far away, as though through a tunnel.

"S'gana!" Derek called over and over, as he entered the stadium from the back and ran down the center aisle. She was in the main show tank. A sling had been fitted around her body with holes cut out for her pectoral fins. Several divers guided her body toward the stage. Doc Barnes kneeled at the edge of the stage, her medicine bag beside her. Shots. S'gana hated them. It seemed to Derek that she ought to be struggling, putting up a fight, but all he saw was an occasional flip of her tail.

"No!" Derek cried, as he took the steps two at a time. "You're going to kill her!"

Doc Barnes paused. "Of course I'm not going to kill her. She has an infection. I'm giving her antibiotics." With all his strength, Derek threw himself against the glass retaining wall, but as soon as he felt the cold pain in his arms, he was grabbed from behind. Two strong arms pulled him back. Several others grabbed his legs and his middle.

"Let her go!" he shouted at them, struggling as they carried him to a golf cart parked just outside the stadium. "What has she ever done to you?"

That night Derek awoke to a voice speaking, *Look for her under the moon.* Was it really a voice? Or a fragment of a dream? Then he sensed Ilyea's presence. The memory of S'gana's body seeped back in, like smoke through a crack beneath the door. Derek fought them both—Ilyea and the vision. He wanted sleep, he wanted to forget, but Ilyea wouldn't let him. *Look for her under the moon,* the voice within him repeated.

Later Derek would remember everything. He sat up quietly and untangled the sheets from around his feet. At the door, the air that met him was surprisingly cool and tangy with salt. The old back steps bowed under his weight, creaking like a docked boat at its moorings. The moon had washed a foamy tide of light across the backyard. Derek stood blinking into its brightness. Over in the garden, Derek saw her.

It seemed as though a piece of the moon had broken free and come to rest on her head, its patient light streaming through the cracks of her woven spruce hat and cedar rain cape, and glinting off the copper and bone necklaces that swung heavily from her neck.

When he reached the bottom step, she turned toward him, shafts of light dancing over the darkened yard with each shift of her form. Neither of them moved closer. S'gana reached out to him, but Derek understood at once that it was not an invitation. His burning eyes closed and he felt the night go black. When he opened them, rubbing away the tears, S'gana was gone. The yard was again dark and ordinary. The moon was covered by scudding clouds.

Derek sat down heavily on the step. He didn't need Ocean Park to confirm it. S'gana was dead. A numbness came over him, as if he'd been walking for days and even one more step would be too much. He stared into the darkness, listening to the sound of Tani's wind chimes in the rising wind.

Derek felt a tap on his shoulder. He turned around, but no one was there. He put his hand out, and after a moment felt a warm drop of rain on his palm. The rain spattered the back of his neck, his cheeks, his knees, with cool kisses. Was she really still with him?

Then he knew: the rain was a gift from S'gana, a gift to the town's children and their parents, who would have saved her had they been given enough time.

The rain fell harder, hammering the sidewalks, the driveways, and the roofs. Derek heard windows thrown open, and the excited talk of the neighbors.

"Derek?" Joe called from the top step. The light from Derek's room outlined his grandfather's body, his rain-soaked nightshirt clinging to his skin. Slowly, Derek made his way up the steps.

"Are you all right, son?" Joe asked, taking him by the shoulders and pulling him inside. "Did you have a bad dream?"

"S'gana's dead, Joe." Derek pressed his face against his grandfather's body.

"It's all right," Joe said, throwing a towel around him. "It was just a dream."

"No!" Derek cried. "No, it wasn't. I saw her."

"But you've seen her before."

"This was different."

"Shush, Joe." Tani took Derek's hand and sat him on the bed. She peeled off his wet pajama top and rubbed the coarse towel against his skin and through his hair.

"What did she look like?" she asked Derek softly.

"She was made of light, Tani. But I could see her, too. She looked . . . Haida."

"She wore the cape and the rain hat?"

Derek nodded.

Tani searched in Derek's dresser until she found underwear and pajamas. "She's home now, Derek," she said, handing him the dry things. Then, taking Joe by the arm, Tani left the room. Derek was glad they understood that he wanted to be alone. There was nothing left to say. He picked up the clothes from the bed and went into the bathroom to dry off and change.

Derek stayed a long while in bed the next morning. Though he was exhausted, sleep seemed far away. And yet, for the first time in weeks, he had no reason to get up. Nothing he could do or say today would make a difference. S'gana was dead. Somewhere, far off, he heard a phone ring. Life would go on, he thought bitterly, just as if S'gana never existed.

Derek heard a soft knock on the door. As it creaked open, he shut his eyes, hoping that whoever it was would go away. He felt someone sit down on the mattress.

Tani took his hand in hers. "You have to grieve," she said slowly. "You should grieve. But don't think of her death as your failure. That would be giving yourself too much power." She sat quietly for a moment before getting up to leave. "Theresa wants you to call."

How do you grieve? Derek wondered after she left. He tried to remember an emptiness like this. It wasn't so much S'gana's presence that he missed—after all, they'd only spent a few short hours together—it was the promise of her. A world with S'gana was full of possibilities. When she was alive, he and Ilyea had worked together as one. With S'gana dead, everything seemed cold and divided. Adults against children, animals against people.

She had made him see that he could do anything he felt was right. If this world really belonged to the past, then Derek agreed with Kwung. He, too, was living in the wrong time.

Twelve

J-7

Derek welcomed the cold, salty breeze that stung his cheeks as the ferry made its way to Eagle Cove, the port closest to Del Arvayo's orca research station. When he heard about S'gana's death, Del had invited them all to visit, but Joe had to stay behind for the fair, and Theresa had to make plans for her future before taking any trips. Derek closed his eyes and leaned his head against Tani's broad shoulder, letting himself be lulled by the rocking motion of the ferry.

Ocean Park had held a memorial service for "Katy," which none of them attended. In the newspaper it said the park was "committed to further research to help man understand orcas." If only they had believed in S'gana, Derek thought, she could have taught them more about black whales than they had ever dreamed possible.

At Tani's suggestion, Reverend Elsley spoke about S'gana in his Sunday sermon. He said some nice things about how she had brought people together and how she had inspired those who knew her, but it wasn't enough. Reverend Elsley didn't know the S'gana that Derek knew. For all his fine words, he couldn't describe her, or give Derek any hope of finding her again. And Derek wanted more than anything to find her again, even if it was not the way he'd known her before.

Derek thought sadly of the body she'd left behind, her graceful markings, her proud dorsal fin. She was still at Ocean Park. Theresa said they would perform an autopsy on her to determine why she died. But what would they do with her when they were through? She deserved to be in the ocean, in the Village-Below-the-Sea, but Derek doubted she would ever make it back there to be buried.

A man brushed by Derek in a stiff orange slicker and grabbed a fat coil of rope on the deck. The warning bell sounded. They were getting close to port.

Derek could barely make out Eagle Cove through the fog that encircled them. Graying piers were lined with fishing boats that rose and fell with the waves. He held Tani's hand as they stepped onto the dock.

"Derek?" A slight man in a long-sleeved shirt, jeans, and a baseball cap approached them. He took Derek's cold hand between both of his. "I'm Del Arvayo." The ocean splashed against the dock, seeping into the ruffle of Tani's denim skirt. She gathered the material together with one hand and shook Del's hand with the other.

"You must be Tani," he said. She nodded. They looked at each other in silence for a moment before Del led the way down the swaying pier. Derek stopped to look back. Already the fog had closed off any view of the ocean beyond the cove. They followed Del to a small fishing boat, and Derek helped him loosen the ropes from the dock.

"Potlatch Island isn't far," Del explained, "but it has no ferry service. You see, I lease the land from a timber company, so I'm the only one who lives there." The fishing boat was more affected by the waves than the ferry had been, and Derek began to feel a little queasy once they left the bay. He tried to steady himself by grabbing the iron railing at the prow.

After about twenty minutes, Del moored the boat in a small bay. "This is Potlatch Island," he said. "Home to many more whales than humans."

"Fine with me," came Derek's quiet reply.

A short pier led up to the water's edge. At the back of the clearing sat a two-story cabin. Beyond that was a wall of giant cedars.

Derek had trouble standing in the boat as he handed the luggage and Del's supplies onto the pier. "I've lost my sea legs," he whispered to Tani, but she didn't hear him.

Ever since they had left Eagle Cove, she seemed preoccupied. Tani walked slowly up the pier, taking in every detail of the island. "Everything rushes back," she whispered to Derek, smiling. "No matter how long you're gone."

Tani was right. Everything was rushing back for him, too. All kinds of memories—hauling in the heavy, squirming nets with his father, picnicking with his mother on Hansen's bluff, searching for tidepools. But there were deeper memories, too, of snowcapped mountain peaks and low, white sheets of clouds.

Derek had a chance to explore the cabin while Del and Tani changed clothes. The large, high-ceilinged room on the first floor had a big fireplace on one side and a bank of windows overlooking the bay on the other. An old sofa, chair, and coffee table faced the fireplace. In the corner was a large desk covered with nautical charts and dated notebooks. Beside it, set into a bookcase, was a stereo system with big speakers.

Upstairs, there were only two rooms. Tani and Derek's had the same high windows as the front room below. Del's was smaller, with a narrow cot against the window and some snapshots tacked to the wall above his dresser.

Derek went downstairs to sit next to the fire. He gazed out at the darkening sky and the first stars of the evening.

"If you like, I can start dinner now," Del said. Tani and Derek offered to help, then realized there wasn't room for the three of them in the small kitchen.

Soon Del had set dishes of rice, beans, warmed tortillas, and chopped vegetables on the coffee table, and given everyone a plate. Derek watched carefully as Del spooned one ingredient after another in thin lines down the center of his tortilla. Before rolling it up, he added a few spoonfuls of red sauce from a jar at his side.

"This is my mother's special salsa," Del said, passing the jar around the table. "She sends it to me by the case." Derek began spooning rice and beans onto his own tortilla, but when he got to the salsa, Del took hold of his wrist.

"Careful," he said, "it takes some getting used to. Taste it first." Derek licked the spoon and immediately his tongue burned. Both Tani and Del were watching him to see how he would react. Derek wished they'd stop. He picked up his water glass slowly, taking just a little sip.

"Isn't it hard sometimes, to live here alone?" he asked Del.

"Hard?" Del flashed a grin. "No. If anything, it's too easy."

"Why?" Derek asked, rolling his tortilla the way he had seen Del do.

"Because I understand the whales, and they understand me. It's not that way with humans."

"It's not easy to get to know a human," Derek said, before he realized he was using S'gana's words.

When the dishes had been cleared, Del disappeared into the kitchen again. Derek got up to help, but Tani held his arm.

"He likes working alone," she said. Del came back in with a punchbowl in one hand and three coffee cups in the other. When he set the bowl down, Derek could see slices of lemons, oranges, and cherries floating in a dark liquid. Del got a bottle from the bookshelf and poured it over the fruit. Then he lit a fireplace match and held it above the bowl. A flame danced over the liquid.

"Café flambé," he said, ladling the drinks into cups as soon as the fire had died down. "To celebrate your visit." He smiled shyly and sat down.

It was the most wonderful drink Derek had ever tasted. Del told him it had coffee, apple cider, and sugar in it along with the fruit and brandy.

"Can we sit outside on the pier?" Derek asked, when Del offered them a second cup. He brought them all blankets to ward off the wet, chilly air.

The clouds moved quickly over the surface of the moon. When they cleared, there was a beautiful show of stars and the moon lit a path across the water.

"Look." Tani pointed to the sky. "A falling star."

Derek caught the last moment of fire before it burned out. He told them about the night he saw the falling star and how he finally understood what S'gana had meant about starting with Tani, the person most likely to believe in her. Then he pulled his whale carving from his pocket. "We couldn't have done it without this," Derek said, handing it to Del.

Del examined the little whale closely. "Do you mind telling me the whole story? From the beginning?" he asked. Derek glanced at Tani. They hadn't spoken much about their attempt to rescue S'gana since she died. But Del deserved to know what had brought them here.

"The very beginning?" Derek asked him. Del nodded, and Derek took a deep breath. "Well, all my life I've felt like I was two boys. . . ."

The next day, Tani and Derek came downstairs to find Del sitting at his desk, already at work. Tani poured herself some coffee. Remembering how good the coffee had been the night before, Derek said he wanted some, too, but the first sip tasted horrible, just like his mom's. Tani warmed some milk and mixed a drink for Derek that was half coffee and half milk. Then she added sugar.

"This is how I learned to drink it," she said. Derek found the second version much better, but still took only small sips. They went over to Del's desk.

"When I left my job at the university to observe orcas in the wild," Del explained, spreading out a chart before them, "I chose Potlatch Island as my base because it is one of the last islands in the strait between mainland Canada and Vancouver Island. A lot of orcas pass through here on their way to the warmer, calmer waters.

"Starting around the end of June, the pods return to the calmer waters to bear their young. I do my recording during the summer." Del pulled one of his notebooks down from the shelf above him. He showed Tani and Derek how he used a separate letter for each pod to keep track of their migratory patterns.

"I'm pretty sure that S'gana was a member of J pod. I called her J–11. She had a slight curve at the tip of her dorsal fin that helped me recognize her. J–11 disappeared right around the time I read that a female orca who fit her description was captured by Ocean Park at Pender Harbour."

"Did J–11 ever give birth?" Tani asked him.

"I would only know that if I recorded a calf to her." Del ran his finger along a row of figures. "And I didn't. But it seems to me that a number of whales from her pod, including a very persistent male I call J–7, were present during the entire time she was being held in Pender Harbour. I remember him well because he had a deep incision on his dorsal fin, which he probably got from a boat motor."

"Do you ever see J pod anymore?" Derek asked.

"They're a resident pod, which means that they call this strait home, at least during the summer months. But I haven't seen them this summer."

"Do you think we could find them?" Derek asked.

But Del didn't seem to be listening. "S'gana is a much nicer name than J–11," he said, as he rechecked his figures. "Maybe I should change the way I name the whales."

"Maybe they passed by at night," Tani said, looking out the window toward the choppy waters of the bay, "and you missed them."

"I confess, I do sleep," Del admitted, laughing, "but

I manage to record most of them." He explained how he had set up underwater microphones in the strait so that whenever a pod passed through, their vocalizations would be broadcast in his living room. Then he would rush to a nearby bluff to record the whales.

"I can identify whole pods now by their dorsal fins," he said proudly. "Sometimes I take my kayak and paddle out to join them."

Derek asked Del if he and Tani could go out with him.

"I thought you might want to," Del said, "so I borrowed a two-man—or two-person, I should say—kayak from a friend of mine. I have to do a wire check on my underwater microphones today. If you like, we can go after breakfast."

Both Del and Derek looked at Tani, but a burst of loud whistling and clicking came over the loudspeaker, drowning out her answer. The noise was so high and shrill it made Tani and Derek cover their ears.

"Sorry!" Del shouted, as he reached over to adjust the sound. "It was still set on night volume." The whistles died down to a less painful level.

He grabbed his notebook and a pair of binoculars, and led them outside to a narrow path through the trees and up to the bluff he had told them about earlier. At the top they could see the entire strait and the whale pod that was moving quickly toward the mouth of it.

"That's B pod," Del told them, after examining the whales through his binoculars. He handed them to Derek, and began making notations in his book. "Can you see the new calf?" Near the rear of the group, two black whales were lagging behind. The dorsal fin of the calf that swam between them was no bigger than a dolphin's. Though he didn't want to give them up, Derek handed the binoculars to Tani. They watched the pod until it was out of sight, then went inside to eat breakfast.

Afterward, they collected the microphones, wiring, and kayaks from Del's storage shed. They loaded the equipment into the kayaks through the small hole where the paddler sat, and carried them down to the end of the pier.

"They're so light," Derek said.

"It's because they're made out of fiberglass," Del told him.

Tani passed around the life jackets she had brought down from the shed. "When I was a girl, I saw an Inuit kayak. They made theirs from driftwood and sealskin, even lighter than this."

"These kayaks are patterned after the Indian ones, with a wide bottom and sharp prow so they don't rock as you cut through the waves," Del explained. "When you get in and fasten the skirt around you, almost no water can get in, so they're really very efficient transportation."

After they had put on their life jackets, Del dropped Tani and Derek's kayak into the water and held it steady with a tow rope as they lowered themselves in. Tani untied the rope while Derek kept their kayak steady by holding onto a piling. Del lowered his own kayak between theirs and the pier, then got in.

They pushed off from the dock, and Del had them paddle several times around the protected cove to get the hang of kayaking. The glassy water made Derek feel like a water bug skating across the surface.

As soon as they were out in the strait, however, the water got choppy. Derek kept trying to slice into the water with his paddle, as Del had instructed, but the swells would raise the kayak up and he would miss the surface entirely. It was a relief to have Tani in front. She was having a hard time paddling, too, but she still acted like everything was under control.

Del headed for what seemed to be a buoy, but Derek could only catch glimpses of it between the rise and fall of the water.

"That must be the marker for the underwater microphones," Derek had to shout in order to be heard over the wind and the water. When they reached it, Del roped himself to the buoy and hauled up several cables. Then he took his extra microphone and wired it to the others. Derek's teeth began to chatter. He was nearly soaked.

"Done," Del said, pushing his wet hair off his face.

Back at the cabin, they changed into dry clothes. Del spent the rest of the afternoon contacting friends on his ham radio, trying to locate J pod. While Tani rested, Derek went back to the bluff Del used for sighting. Del would join him there every time a pod of orcas passed through the strait. Derek loved to watch them go by, diving and breaching. He couldn't tell whether they were playing or fishing. What difference did it make? It was all the same thing.

That night Derek lay awake, wondering about S'gana. It didn't make any sense for her to appear to him in human form again. There was nothing he could do for her now. But wasn't that really what he'd wanted in coming here? That, or a sign telling him she was all right, that she'd made it home.

It was a long time before he fell asleep.

Look for her under the moon. For the second time in a week, Derek awoke to see himself lying among tangled sheets. This time, he did not question the call to go out, but slipped quietly from his bunk and dressed, putting his whale carving in his pocket.

The moon shone through the quickly moving clouds like a lighthouse beacon, one moment bathing the earth and the water with light, the next plunging them into darkness.

Something was calling him back to the buoy that Del had taken them to earlier. He walked carefully down the pier and stared into the darkness. How would he find it? He was aware of the wind rushing through the pipe railing and the trees behind him. He listened. *Ilyea, the great fisherman whose spirit is in you, used the stars and the moon to guide him. The two of you are one,* an inner voice reminded him.

Derek felt his way up the path to the storage shed to get one of Del's kayaks and a paddle. He carried them down to the dock and dropped the boat into the water as he had seen Del do. Knotting the tow rope around a piling, he lowered himself into the kayak and loosened the cord from the boat. Derek tried to dip his paddle smoothly into the water as the kayak began to roll with the waves. Soon he was making headway.

But where? During the day, waves had made the bright orange buoy hard to see. Now it was so dark he couldn't make out the line between sea and sky. When the moon broke through and traced a path along the water, Derek began working his way toward the light, pulling hard to make some progress against the tide.

Soon a thick patch of fog surrounded him, blotting out the comforting lights of the cabin. The only sound was the slapping of water all around him. Alone with his thoughts, Derek began to wonder if he'd done the right thing. But there was no turning back now.

Finally, when he was sure he couldn't dip the paddle into the water one more time, the fog lifted slightly and Derek spied the orange buoy, bobbing on the water just ahead of him. He made his way toward it, pulling with everything he had. Then the clouds covered up the moon, and once again he could no longer see clearly.

Derek stopped to rest and immediately felt the pull of the tide dragging him off course. He didn't have the strength to fight it. He looked back toward the shore, but saw nothing. Tani and Del were still asleep, unaware that he'd even left the house. He reached beneath the water skirt for the little whale in his pocket.

As soon as he had it in his palm, Derek felt a presence. It was only a sensation at first, but when he heard a soft whoosh of breath, he understood. A whale was nearby. He heard several more bursts of air and realized that whales surrounded him. When the clouds revealed the moon again, he saw the shapes of their backs and the silhouettes of their dorsal fins gliding through the waves.

They had come, ready to listen, but how could he communicate with these huge creatures? Derek closed his eyes and concentrated on his carving, pressing his numb fingers over its familiar contours. Silently, he repeated the name *S'gana* over and over, until he could picture her. It was with this image that he spoke to them. He had come to ask about his friend, S'gana, and whether she'd found her way back to the Village-Below-the-Sea.

When Derek opened his eyes, he could see that the whales had moved closer, knitting themselves into such a tight pattern around him that it seemed he could crawl out of his kayak and across their backs. He forgot about S'gana for a moment and stared at them in wonder. But as soon as he did this, the whales broke their woven pattern and, circling his boat, they submerged, leaving him spinning in the whirlpool they had created.

"Wait!" Derek called. "Please!" The kayak, which had been safe and still surrounded by the pod of whales, was once more pulled by the tide. He searched the glistening water for a sign that the whales were still near, but he could see nothing. He was too tired to go after them. His search for S'gana would have to wait.

The current on the return trip was much stronger,

pitching his boat back and forth so that his arms got tired after just a few strokes. What little progress he made was soon lost to the tide. The fog had lifted somewhat, but the clouds still covered the moon, making it hard for him to find his way.

Suddenly, from behind him, a huge swell lifted his kayak. Slowly, gently, the boat turned over, and Derek found himself pinned underneath it. Cold, black water swirled around his head, numbing his whole body. He tried to free himself from the water skirt that held him in the kayak, but his movements were clumsy and his lungs screamed for air. He clawed at the water, but there was nothing to hold onto.

"S'gana," he pleaded, kicking free of the boat, "help me!" Then his body took over, sucking in water as if it were air, and he began to cough violently.

Derek felt something brush against him. It rose to his side and he grabbed for it, realizing it was his only chance to be saved. He held on with all his strength, but it was so huge that as they approached the surface, it began to lift him right out of the water. His hands slid down the massive fin, and he felt the deep notch at the base.

"J–7," he whispered, just before passing out.

Listen. Crickcrickcrick. A high-pitched noise over there.

Voices cry out to Derek through the darkness. Two legs become one. He flicks his powerful tail. His arms grow, shoulders join his head, rounding out his body. He is warm all over.

Crickcrickcrick. Where am I? *The answer echoes back. Deep reef, sandy bottom, Village-Below-the-Sea. Black bodies glide past, smoothing, rubbing, pushing him toward the surface.*

Breathe, silly. A familiar voice rolls over him. Air rushing out the top of his head, tingling, a fine mist settles on his back. He glides through the water, rubbing against pebbles on the ocean floor, feeding on salmon. The whales rest close together. Then, spyhopping across the surface of the water, he sees a light in the distance. A figure on the dock, Kitkune, his grandmother, singing. Below, he sends another message. The whales breathe out, sighing. Home.

When Del first heard the whales calling to each other over the speakers, he slipped out of bed and through the darkness with practiced ease. It wasn't until he was on his way back from the bluff that he saw Tani standing at the edge of the pier in her nightgown, singing to the wind.

"Tani." Del touched her gently on the shoulder, but she did not respond.

In the moonlight her face had a faraway look,

almost as if she were in a trance. Her lips moved silently. Then Del saw the tow rope, and he shined his flashlight along the nylon cord until he lost it in the water. He ran up the path to the storage shed and found his kayak missing. Back in the cabin, Del lit every lamp he owned so that Derek would be able to find his way home. Then he grabbed a heavy blanket and took it down to the pier. When he approached Tani, she waved him away. Confused, Del again offered her the blanket. She shook her head slightly. Was she praying?

Derek woke up, shivering. His face was pressed against something wet and cold. As he came to, he began to remember what had happened. He felt along the long dorsal fin until his hands reached the deep ridge.

"Then it's true. You are J–7!" In the distance, Derek could see the blazing lights of the cabin.

"I've got to get back," he said. But how? He'd lost his kayak and his paddle. J–7 sank down a few inches and began to glide through the water, his dorsal fin cutting into the choppy waves. Derek held tight as the saltwater stung his eyes.

They sailed across the water toward land. The whale stopped about fifty feet from the pier, and Derek understood this was as far as he would go.

"Good-bye," he whispered, rubbing the whale's

flank, "and thank you." J–7 slapped his tail loudly on the surface before diving beneath the water. Derek stroked through the cold water quickly, shouting to Tani and Del.

"Derek," Tani said over and over, as she embraced her grandson. Del threw the blanket over his shoulders.

"It's true, isn't it, Tani?"

"Yes," Tani said, hugging him. "S'gana's spirit is nearby, protecting us."

"That was S'gana's son, I'm sure of it," Derek told them.

They looked out into the bay and, in the gray light of dawn, watched a black whale leap clear out of the water and dive gracefully below the surface. Then he blew a tall, fine spray of water high into the air before swimming to the mouth of the bay and back to his mother in the Village-Below-the-Sea.

Acknowledgments

I offer my sincerest thanks to the following people: the dear friends and fellow writers who see me through, Jo Anne Behling, Patricia Blanco, Judy Elsley, Valerie Martinez, Amy Pence, and Susan Roberts; my sisters, Ann Hutchins and Cary Stauffacher; my early, enthusiastic readers, Beth, Ferdie, Kathryn, and Michael Alvarado, and Huntley Cooney; my agent, Tim Schaffner, for heeding the call to "Go West" to bring S'gana back to the sea; my editors Jeffrey Lockridge, whose diligent work helped me transform my manuscript into a novel, and Brenda Peterson, whose encouraging critique helped me to polish it; the staffs at Harbinger House and Alaska Northwest Books for believing in this project; and finally, to Tim Hurd, Paul Spong, and Irma and Herb Stauffacher, whose lives have inspired characters in this book.

About the Author

Author Sue Stauffacher teaches English at the University of Arizona. While attending college, she worked seasonally for three years at a marine park—an experience that inspired her to write this book.

She is currently an artist-in-residence in creative writing and storytelling for the state of Arizona, in Tucson, where she lives with her husband and son. *S'gana, The Black Whale* is her first novel for young readers.

Readers of S'GANA, THE BLACK WHALE won't want to miss our other exciting books for young readers:

RING OF TALL TREES, by John Dowd.
Dylan and his Native friends call on Native ritual to help save a stand of ancient trees from being logged.
Hardbound, 128 pages, $14.95, ISBN 0-88240-398-2

THE WAR CANOE, by Jamie S. Bryson.
Mickey Church, a defiant Tlingit youth from Wrangell, Alaska, sees a vision of his proud Tlingit forebears and a fabled war canoe that changes his life.
Softbound, 198 pages, $9.95, ISBN 0-88240-368-0

ONCE UPON AN ESKIMO TIME, by Edna Wilder, with illustrations by Dorothy Mayhew.
Once Upon an Eskimo Time tells the story of a year in a young Eskimo girl's life at Rocky Point village on the Bering Sea Coast before the white man came. With 22 illustrations.
Softbound, 204 pages, $12.95, ISBN 0-88240-274-9

THE EYE OF THE CHANGER, by Muriel Ringstad, with illustrations by Donald Croly.
A tale of life on Puget Sound long ago, *The Eye of the Changer* tells of a Salish boy's ventures among the elements and the spirits. With 70 illustrations.
Softbound, 96 pages, $9.95, ISBN 0-88240-251-X

Ask for these books at your favorite bookstore, or contact Alaska Northwest Books™ for a complete catalog.

Alaska Northwest Books™
A division of GTE Discovery Publications, Inc.
P.O. Box 3007, Bothell, WA 98041-3007
1-800-331-4567